The Famine Village

Also by Georg Engel from K A Nitz:

Thy Neighbour's Wife

The Famine Village

Georg Engel

K A Nitz

WELLINGTON

Das Hungerdorf first published
in German 1893

This translation into New Zealand English
Copyright © K A Nitz 2014
All rights reserved

ISBN: 978-0-473-28182-3

Contents

THE FAMINE VILLAGE

*No mother doubts at the bottom of her heart that
she has given birth to a possession in the child.*
Friedrich Nietzsche.

Hesitating, trembling, as it were with liquid fervour, the sinking sun was lingering for a moment yet on the outermost blue edge of the sea.

Then one more last, ardent, yearning look at the small Baltic island over whose forests it was rolling past in the morning, one more last trembling beam on the miserable, impoverished fishing settlement there in the midst of the stony cleft — and across the still surface of the water went a shudder, and the defeated star plunged down into the dim blue, unending bed.

On the stony beach, meanwhile, stood an aged, squalidly dressed woman, and she looked sharply across the sea as it gleamed in colours, as if she were trying to seek something, spy out something out there.

On her arm, the woman carried a basket from which a quite fine, barely visible steam was rising, and it suggested that the old woman had placed a just cooked meal in the woven basket. And the finer and more whitish the cloud became, the more frequently the pinched, sharp grey eyes of the basket carrier strayed back from the sea to her burden, the more unwillingly and impatiently she lifted the woven basket to her hook-like nose to breath in the emanating aroma vexedly and hungrily as well.

At the same time, her deeply shrunken mouth opened, revealing a small number of teeth standing individually, and her conspicuously narrow, bloodless lips murmured a few furious words.

Five steps closer to the sea, an old fisherman in shirtsleeves and ragged trousers, his bare feet stuck into crude wooden clogs, sat on an upturned boat, and was hammering with all his might a rectangular board firmly onto one of the ribs. With his work, the old man whistled incessantly to himself always the four high and four low bars until his companion finally stepped up to him, and pulled on his loosely hanging neckerchief.

"Well, what then, my little cuckoo?" the fisherman asked as he turned his fat, red face to her, and propped the handle of his hammer forcefully on the boat.

"My boy isn't back," the mother lamented anxiously, "the wind has surely turned around since he took the stranger to Cona."

And again the patiently waiting woman swept her gaze across the calm, redly glowing surface while the mariner shook his head critically — then yet one timidly shrewd look up into the averted, wrinkled countenance of the woman, and he dipped his fat finger deftly into the steaming pot which the woman was carrying on her arm, and then licked it off furtively.

"Potato soup with sausages — eh!"

"What?" the old woman asked in astonishment.

The fisherman stuck his hands comfortably in his pockets, and licked his lips.

"Yes," he concurred, blinking, "your Klas will probably not return today. There is a dance in the Cona tavern tonight — there the tigers will be skipping about the maids the whole night through — always one, two, three, one, two, three; Scottish and ballroom waltzes that give me gout if I just think of them. Why not?" he added mockingly and with a certain gloating joy. — "Klas must go amongst the women for once, he has sat by himself now quite long enough, my black-haired Hanne, right, my little hen, my little cuckoo, my little cuckoo?"

The old woman threw a sharp, blazing look at the speaker as if she wanted to give him a vehement answer, but she overcame herself and just grumbled dissatisfied, "Each should return to his own threshold! What concern of yours is my Klas? Have you perhaps raised him up and protected him? No, I did it, and for that he must now take care of me until I have shut my eyes. Should I perhaps starve now when the herring catch has stopped completely? Haven't you read yet in the Bible what is said about the mother there? Well, that's by the by, you are always drunk anyway."

"No," the affronted man whined, as the offended mother turned again to the sea so as to more longingly penetrate the rosy evening veil. "No, not entirely — I can still distinguish quite well a jealous little woman from an old witch. Well, now don't bark again, and regarding your Klas, he has something going on with my brunette Mieke — a strapping lass too — sparkling done up — if you could have seen them both yesterday behind the barn, well —"

The talker stroked his chin smugly.

"We were like that once also, Hanne, you know, when I beset you; it was a handsome time, and then you suddenly disposed of me, and married your Jochen. God bless him — it was a nasty affair — you could have had me!"

The ragged fisherman shook his head agitatedly, and still seemed piqued today about the girlfriend of his youth making such a bad decision at the time; the black-haired Hanne, however, walked up to him, and furiously stretched her frail hand out towards him.

And there was none of the former tenderness to be seen, no, her wrinkled mouth instead spewed a flood of abuse towards her admirer, and screamed and nagged about how he could allow himself to speak of Mieke and her Klas, the old pimp, him — and her son had to maintain his mother, just her — but what would such a drunkard know about that; and just as she was in the middle of the wildest scolding, her old lover grasped his hammer, and began banging away ear-numbingly on his board.

Louder and louder and ever louder until it sounded like a light cannonade, and at the same time, he spoke with beautiful calm just four words in accompaniment, "angry devil — house dragon."

And again, "house dragon — angry devil!" until the old woman lost her breath, lifted her basket up with a furious sideways glance, and ran off in fury to her little cottage lying higher up.

But the cannonade continued, and only when the last trace of a basket and a woman's skirt had vanished behind the stony cleft did the fisherman prop his hammer demurely on his knee, and reflectively shake out a little heap of the soft golden sand from his wooden clogs, "Pity," he murmured, "she had hair at the time as — as black as a raven's, and eyes as grey and bright as, hm, hm — —"

No fitting comparison occurred to the old man, and hence he decided shortly, "She had eyes alright, and if I had gotten her at the time, I would not perhaps have become such a ragged dawdler with not a pfennig in my pocket, and patching up other people's boats. But I just did not get her and hence — ups-a-daisy, hooray!" —

And the old dilapidated man-child began singing loudly so that the individual notes sounded far across the sea.

The Famine Village

At the same time, a boat was gliding towards the wretched fishing settlement.

Hardly a stone's throw from the forested coast, it drew past ponderously, and the faint evening wind was barely capable of imparting any curve to the slack sails. You could distinctly make out the twittering and piping of the birds singing themselves to sleep in the dark coastal forest, a strong smell of wood and sap came across, and the silver beams of the rising moon revealed already the light mist striking out from the forest.

In the boat, however, sat Klas, the son of the black-haired Hanne, her pride, her breadwinner, her last love, and he held the sail rope attentively in his large calloused hand.

He had turned his hulking, sandy-haired head to the land, and his deep-set, shy blue eyes peered with a dull, dreamy look at the white veils which were assuming wondrous forms down there on the spurs of beach scrub.

Was not everything slipping, dancing, and billowing forth there?

Strange, ghostly pale faces looked out from the bushes, white bodies stirred there behind the branches, and between the dark trunks, fleeting, delicate beings were dancing.

"Mist," Klas said apprehensively, "there will be bad weather tomorrow."

He thought about how he would then not be able to set out his nets tomorrow, that he would then earn nothing again, not the few bare pfennigs from which he and his mother could live scantily, nothing at all yet again.

Klas took the sail down, and propped his head in both hands.

What a life over there in the wretched village!

Everyone residing in the small settlement was exposed daily to starvation.

For years already, the fishing had as good as stopped, the fin bearers were fleeing this part of the coast, and neither craft nor prayer was capable of enticing them into the empty nets.

In summer, things still worked out at least.

Then a tourist sometimes came to the village, and had himself ferried to Cona.

It brought a few groschen at least. But in winter, when the icy blizzard stormed over the island, when the rickety wooden shacks in which the fishermen lived were shaken up so that the snow swept through all the cracks, what would become of him in winter, of him and his frail old mother?

"Yes, yes," the poor fellow sighed, "it is very bad."

And then he thought again of something else.

Had he only not gone to the tavern that time a month ago when he received a shiny taler from a tourist.

But his mother had wanted him to, and he had gone there, and seen her dancing, Mieke, the most beautiful girl in the entire village, he had seen her whirling about in a strange, rocking, city dance, and her skirt had rustled and clung closely around her broad hips, and she had nodded to him over the shoulder of her partner so wildly, so lightheartedly.

And she had also wanted to whirl around with him, but he had not known the dance, and had been laughed at, and she had laughed along. Only he led her home that evening, they had walked quite alone through the darkness, yes, her breast was still flying up and down from the last, ardent dance, and hence they had not spoken a word to each other until they had arrived at the house of her father, the old ragged and dilapidated boat mender Jochen Wulkow.

They called him Mad Johann in the village, because of the turbid, mad talk which schnaps endowed him with; the place in which he resided with Mieke was an unusable, tiny smokehouse, shaped like a beehive, made from clay, with large seams and cracks and a burst roof.

Here Klas had held his companion, and stroked her full, round arm timidly, almost bewilderedly with his thick hand.

He had not dared further caresses. It was also the first time that a woman other than his mother had seemed worth a glance to him, and the girl had chided him, and laughingly said, "You can be my sweetheart, Klas, adieu."

Since then the wild thing had forced herself into his vicinity, teased and mocked him, and he dreamt of her, and thought of her.

"Hey!"

The sail flapped slackly against the mast so that the helmsman rose his hulking head, and now satisfied himself that the wind had died off completely. The boat had floated quite close to the forest topped dunes, and when Klas now rose to tie the sail to the mast, it seemed as if a white figure detached itself from the mists which cloaked the beach; through the moonlight and evening mist, a white, voluptuous, gleaming figure rose out of the lapping water, then remained standing motionless in her shimmering brilliance on the damp sand, and suddenly vanished jubilantly between the moonlit trees.

Klas had distinctly, quite distinctly heard the wild shout, his practiced ear had quite clearly distinguished the splattering and lapping of the water, yes, even the fluttering hair of the mermaid had not escaped his gaze.

Those damp, gleaming limbs, all enveloped by the heavy, white mists, those thick strands of dripping hair on which tiny blue sparks had danced, they could not have belonged to any earthly woman.

No, no — and the superstitious fellow rubbed his forehead — that was the kind of cold-blooded mermaid about which the old fishermen so often told tales, a mermaid who had taken a liking to him, and had now risen up in Mieke's image to entice him with her into the tepid, endless depths.

He stood their motionless for almost quarter of an hour, and cold shivers ran over his back, but then he took hold of the oars, and strove with all his might to row away from there.

"No, no," he murmured at the same time, "to home, to mother, to home — it all isn't right here."

The boat shot out again into the open sea.

Then a voice echoed across the waters, laughing and enticing, and on one of the giant beach boulders, a dark, supple figure appeared, its skirts fluttering in the evening wind.

"Evening, Klas!"

The oar strokes ceased, but only after a while did an incredulous voice ask, "Mieke, little Mieke — is it you?"

"Well, why wouldn't it be, dumb Klas, don't you know me anymore?"

The poor fellow in the boat shook his hulking head, but then he turned the boat around hastily.

This time it was no illusion. The girl up there was Mieke in flesh and blood, but yet — —

The naked, magical woman who had sprung jubilantly through the evening mist occurred again to the sluggish fellow, and an ardent, fearful passion for her image up there on the boulder took possession of him.

"Well, will it be soon?" the cheeky voice asked from above.

At this moment, the boat crunched onto the sand, and Klas sprang out to wade in his great waterproof boots the short stretch to dry land.

"How goes it, Mieke?" he asked when he was standing next to the boulder, and looked furtively up at her.

The water was still beading from her hair, and Klas stared rigidly at the sparkling drops.

For a moment, it remained quiet between the two, then Klas blinked at the ground, and asked with visible effort, "Mieke — were you — did you — there before? —"

He faltered.

"What?" the girl inquired with a strange, non-committal smile, and kicked the awkward fellow on the arm quite lightly with her wooden clog from her raised seat.

"I — —"

He did not finish. The right words for all that he had felt and seen did not want to glide over his heavy tongue. But as he felt the soft pressure on his arm, that wondrous, magical figure which had risen from the swishing waters and fled into the forest appeared before his foolish eyes again.

"Hey," Mieke began after a while, and threw her hair coquettishly over her shoulder, "did the stranger with whom you sailed to Cona pay well?"

Now Klas awoke, and put his hulking hand into his pocket, "He gave me two ten groschen pieces," he grinned happily, "and a cigar."

"So?!"

Mieke's eyes began to sparkle.

"Klas, you can lift me down," she teased him, and stood up, "but hold me gently."

The luscious, supple figure bent down, and casually placed her arm around his neck.

"Now deftly!" she commanded.

Poor Klas did not know how it happened to him. In the next moment, he had her already in his arms, and as he brought her down in a wide swing, she gave him a lusty kiss with her fresh, red lips.

"You are stupid though," she laughed at the same time, "you must be shown that you are good. Now come though, Klas, we will go home."

And the girl grasped his hand decisively, and attempted to pull him away with her, only the fellow remained standing, and shook his head completely confused, "No, no, first bring the boat onto dry land," he stammered, "you — you."

And then it overpowered him.

With a drunken cry of joy, he plunged onto her, and tried to enclose the brown-haired child in his arms, but she ducked unexpectedly, and eluded him.

"Don't be silly, Klas, and now quick, I want to help you pull in."

With these words, the strong girl grasped one of the boat's lines which lay already on the beach and, supported by the ecstatic fellow, Mieke really brought the little boat after a few minutes onto the sand.

Then the two started on the way home in complete darkness.

When they were in the coastal forest, Mieke began suddenly sobbing softly, and leant her head gently on his shoulder.

Was it the impenetrable night, was it the proximity of the fine, moistly smelling hair which completely intoxicated the poor fellow?

Breathless, full of sympathy, he placed his arm around the crying beauty, and asked with faltering voice, "What is wrong, my dear, sweet Mieke, tell me, what is wrong — can't I help? — Don't cry — dear."

Again he drew her to himself, and this time his words of comfort seemingly worked so consolingly on his pretty companion that she let her coarse sackcloth fall from her damp eyes, and burst out with all the signs of anguish, "Klas, my father has had nothing to eat for two days, the poor, old man — we must starve, I don't like to go home at all anymore."

She remained standing now, and let her head sink down onto her deep breathing chest, yes, Klas thought he noticed despite the darkness that her blooming cheeks were blanched.

The dark, mighty pines rustled and murmured above their heads, and through the heart of the hulking fellow stormed an ardent, aching pity for this sobbing woman.

"Don't cry, Mieke," he requested affectionately, and grasped her hand, "here" — he groped in his pocket — "here, have one of my ten groschen pieces — I want to give it to you, and now be happy again."

He held the coin appeasingly before her eyes; but just as the girl tried to grasp the coin, his hand pulled back once more hesitantly.

"And your old mother?" his inner voice spoke to him, and the low, dimly lit room in which the old woman was waiting for him appeared before him. Had his mother not already made plans that morning for the expected money, and delighted over it?

He pondered and pondered.

Mieke, however, having followed his movements with her large, luminous eyes, became impatient, and pushed his hand back in disappointment.

"Make a fool of another," she said grumbling, "I thought you were better. Leave me in peace."

She tore away vehemently from him, and tried to hurry away.

"Dear, Mieke, Mieke," he cried startled, and ran after her, "don't be angry with me, Mieke, I just want — here, have it — I am really so nice to you," he stammered.

"That is not true, Klas!" Mieke murmured, pocketing the money, and pushed him away anew, "you are lying."

"Really," Klas stammered, and put his hand on his heart in protest.

Mieke nudged him gently with her arm, "Then you are a cheapskate," she said in striding on, "a handsome sweetheart who hasn't gifted his fiance a penny yet!"

"But Mieke, I have nothing though."

"You still have the ten groschen piece in your pocket."

Poor Klas stood still, and rubbed his forehead, "Mieke, that won't work," he protested apprehensively, "that is for my mother at home — we must live."

"Yes well," the beautiful girl said protractedly, and transformed her dark figure with one of her strange looks.

And suddenly she bid him curtly and drily, "Good night."

Klas seized her arm in shock, "Mieke, don't you want to walk with me — — ?"

"No, I can walk alone, let me go," she cried vehemently, and wrested herself from him, "you love only your mother. Go sit with her behind the stove."

Hardly had she spoken the heartless words than she pulled her arms to her breast, and began to flee through the forest.

Klas stood, and stared after her.

Between the moonlit trunks, she again appeared to be the enchanting mermaid with the blue flames above her head and the shimmering limbs.

He was hardly aware of it himself, he had set himself in motion, and was running after the fleeing woman with long strides; but she skimmed along faster and faster, her pursuer was already wheezing, sweat was already appearing on his forehead, then Mieke suddenly paused, and called breathlessly, "What do you want from me? I don't want to have anything to do with you, do you hear?"

Now he stood before her, and wiped the sweat awkwardly from his forehead.

"Here, Mieke," he stammered with a haste as if he were speaking half unconsciously, "here is the money — I am giving you everything that I have, if — you want me to be a bit good to you — just like there under the boulder — where — —"

A bright jubilation interrupted him.

The money had slid into the girl's hand, and she was holding it up in the moonlight so that it sparkled.

It was the same wafting cry which was constantly in Klas's ears, and as he stared numbly at the supple woman, she was already stroking his tousled hair, and kissing his cheeks in tempestuous joy, "You are a good fellow, Klas; you're also my sweetheart who I'll always be fond of, you big, stupid Klas — come."

And she kissed him once more on his wide, trembling lips, gave him a teasing slap on the shoulder, and then scurried in mad haste through the quite steep forest down into the village.

In a few minutes, she had vanished without having looked around once for the man left behind.

A volley of acorns and pine cones falling down from the trees finally woke Klas from his brooding, and reminded him that someone still lived in the village, and surely awaited him anxiously.

He slowly pulled his cloth cap down further over his forehead, and started on the homeward path in pressing thought. Soon he had reached the wretched settlement, and was striding to his own residence without throwing a glance at the two rows of low, dilapidated shacks.

But suddenly he faltered, and pricked up an ear.

To his side lay the round, bursting smoke house in which Mieke lived with her father, the old dawdler

Jochen Wulkow. The light of a burning piece of pine penetrated through the cracks, and the drunken voice of old Mad Johann boomed out loudly into the still night:

> Lovely maiden, pour me,
> Pour me some of the golden wine —

A dull blow as if someone was banging a bottle on the table followed.

Klas stepped back, shaking his head, "A poor, sick man," he murmured depressed, "she has it hard with him."

He dared not think any further, he instead quickened his steps, and soon stood before the threshold of his own, shingle-covered shack.

Here too, dim light shone through the small, barely foot-high window, and when Klas peered timidly through it, he saw how the old woman was sitting at the table before a small candle stump and a covered plate, while her head had sunk slumbering onto the edge of the table.

The view fell heavily on the son's heart.

How tired, how haggard this wrinkled countenance looked — and he?

He instinctively groped in his pocket and sought after the two coins which had shortly before chinked in the coarse lining.

"Mieke, Mieke," he sighed deeply, and he heard again the uncanny cry which the beautiful woman had emitted.

Should he enter now?

Then the door creaked, and the black-haired Hanne raised her nodding head, and tore her tired eyes open.

"Klas, Klas, is it you?" the old woman rasped in hope, and when her son quickly entered, she curiously lifted the plate up, and seemed to be inspecting in particular whether its contents were still edible.

"Quite cold", she rasped with a reproachful look, and drew her shawl tighter about her shoulders, shivering.

"Why did you remain away so long, Klas?"

Her son had seated himself on the bench by the hearth, propped his head on his gnarled fists, and stared fixedly before himself.

This strange silence seemed to be troubling the old woman.

"Are you not well?" she asked with concern, and brushed her fingers over the seated man's strong neck, "are you sick, my boy?"

Her question sounded so fearful, so sympathetic, that it cut the struggling fellow to his heart.

"No, no, mother," he responded, and placed his hand on hers, "I'm just tired."

His mother sighed.

"You work too much," she murmured compassionately, "you must have rowed strongly again? — Well, now take your boots off, my boy, and sit down at the table. I made your favourite meal today because you earned something extra, potato soup with sausages, and I will warm it up now once more. Sit down, Klas."

She busied herself now at the broad hearth, stoked the glimmering wood, and hung the kettle over it; and Klas sat at the crudely built table, and looked into the twitching hearth fire.

In the meantime, the kettle began to bubble, the pieces of wood crackled and burst, and the black-haired Hanne stood next to it and warmed her hands so that the red glow shone through the cracks between her fingers.

"Finished," the old woman said affectionately, and carried the steaming bowl to the table. "Dear, how good that smells. Now eat yourself full, my son."

She sat herself comfortably opposite him, and gazed raptly as he sought out the pieces of sausages with the pewter spoon.

"Tastes good?" she asked after a while.

Did the old woman not notice that her son choked on a few crumbs, that his thoughts did not linger with her, but far below the misty sea?

"Klas, his mother continued gently, "how much have you brought back with you today?"

Klas put the spoon down, for it seemed to him as if he had just felt a real physical pain in his heart.

He stared again into the glimmering wood, and did not stir.

"Well, it is surely not much?" his mother encouraged, although a bleak smile played about her narrow lips.

No answer.

Suddenly, however, Klas slammed his fist on the table, and cried, breaking out in fury at himself, "I have not brought back anything, not a pfennig."

The old woman moved her chair, and tore her eyes open, unbelieving and shocked.

"Nothing?" she repeated slowly, and she instinctively raised her trembling hand. Did he not give you anything?"

Klas looked at his mother glassily, and tried to devise a way out, but the lie would not pass over his heavy tongue.

"No," he wheezed while the sweat broke forth on his forehead, "two ten groschen pieces — I — I gifted them to Mieke —"

"Gifted!? — Klas," the old woman cried hoarsely, and let her shawl slip to the ground, "you are just making that up, aren't you?"

Klas sprang up.

"No, mother, I did it."

"And you will let me starve?" the old woman now shouted, and pounded with her bony finger on the table top, "the entire week only a few pfennigs, and as soon as you have something, you carry it to such a raggedy girl?"

The tears climbed into her eyes so that she lifted her coarse apron up to dry the burning moisture.

"And to such a bad girl," she sobbed with rage, "who associates with all sorts of men. No, that won't end well; listen to your mother, Klas, let the shameful thing run; she is nothing for you, listen to me, Klas, I —"

But the admonition would not be concluded.

Klas had turned to the window, and was staring out into the night with a sombre look. His hands in his trouser pockets, he remained in his place, and dreamt incessantly of the enticing, naked woman whom he overheard down on the beach.

Then something touched his shoulder, and behind him an admonishing voice rang out, "Klas, Klas, listen to me, leave off with the bad thing. We have no bread at home for ourselves, and if you now give such a hussy — —"

The dream was over; the words of the old woman had savagely driven it away. Something like resentment and pique rose in the hulking fellow.

"Klas, you will remain with your old mother, won't you?" the black-haired Hanne sobbed once more, and tried to cling to him, only the fellow shook her off, and turned his back to her petulantly.

"Leave off the crying," he answered curtly, "I can't suffer it."

And without once looking around, he strode ponderously to his room.

It was the first time that the black-haired Hanne had heard a rough word from her son's mouth, and for that reason, she stared after him with wide-open eyes, unable to move. But then she sighed deeply, and slowly cleared the plate and the earthen bowl from the table.

Quarter of an hour later, she was crouching by the low hearth, and had placed in her lap an old, worn Bible whose yellow pages she looked down at through her steel rimmed glasses.

The hearth fire twitched and glowed, heavy drops ran down over the old woman's glasses, and as Hanne followed the broad lines with her forefinger, her lips murmured half mechanically, "Honour thy father and mother, that it may well be with thee, and thou mayest live long on the earth."[1]

And she repeated it three times until she nodded her head after browsing for a long time, and folded her hands devoutly over the book.

Inside his room, Klas lay on the palliasse and dreamt of the flowering woman who had let herself be snatched by him and had pushed him away again, and in the adjoining room, the old woman sat for a long time by the hearth, and what she said was barely understandable, "Give us this day our daily bread — oh, our daily bread, dear God, it is not much — And lead us not into temptation, but deliver us from evil — yes, Mieke, Mieke — she is good for nothing, Klas. — For thine is the kingdom, and the power, and the glory, for ever. Amen."

---

1   Ephesians 6:2.

The Famine Village

It was raining without break, without interruption. The shoots in the earth swelled, and the young seed rotted. And at the same time, a south wind, always a south wind from which the smallest fish fled like from a poisonous breath.

For days the boats lay on the sand and gathered mould. The fishermen sat in their shacks and stopped their grumbling stomachs with half-rotted fish, and the cold, damp rain seeped through the sodden moss on the rooves unhindered into the rooms and down onto the tables and beds.

The last pig was pawned, the last cow slaughtered, with the baker everything unpaid for, lingering illness everywhere, and outside rain, leaden grey rain which swirled incessantly down the miry country road and gave rise to thousands of little bubbles.

It was Sunday.

Through the damp, heavy mist, hollow bell chimes rang out, and called the despairing people to church. They should pray. Perhaps that God up there could finally chase away the mist and bring bread, bread into the house.

Without their usual Sunday best, the coloured overcoat drawn high over the head, the woman waded along; the men followed in their waterproof boots and their woolly fleece jackets, their hands defiantly balled in their pockets.

Klas and the black-haired Hanne were in the midst of them.

In the bare, white-washed church, it smelt of the many drenched clothes.

The woman whispered amongst each other, the men stood in the background, and the damp sand under their boots crunched jarringly on the flagstones.

Above the windows of the house, however, the rain trickled, the rain.

"Hey, boy," old Jochen Wulkow whispered, leaning on the wall next to Klas, and plucked at his coat, "have you ever eaten a roast from a fine deer?"

"No, Jochen," Klas responded, looking tensely out the open door because out there Mieke was standing and chatting casually with a bearded young man in a new green gendarme's uniform.

The gendarme had seized her by the arm, she remained standing smiling before him. It tormented poor Klas.

"Have you ever eaten hare, or turkey, or the tough oysters?" old Mad Johann continued grinning.

"No, Jochen, have you?"

"Eh what, I haven't either, but I think it is all the same whether I have no bread or no roast turkey. Hunger is hunger, don't you think?"

"Yes," Klas agreed, not having understood a word, and only seeing how Mieke strolled with red cheeks through the church door, accompanied constantly by the young gendarme.

The green uniform, the white bandolier, and the clattering sabre made a sensation.

"That is the new gendarme from over in Rohrdorf," the women whispered, but the looks which they threw the handsome man were defiant and unfriendly.

In bad times, the powers that be are not loved.

The policeman in the green coat meanwhile sat down right at the front on a raised seat to the side and stroked his blond moustache with gratification. —

"Yes," the fishermen murmured bitterly, "he receives his steady income, and takes it from out of our pockets."

Then a deep silence occurred. The congregation sang a hymn, at first softly, then louder and louder, and at the end everyone, everyone joined in the chorus, "Our God is a solid castle."

The hymn came to an end, and the rain was heard splattering down again.

The a young clergyman climbed the pulpit, said a short prayer, folded his hands, and looked fervently up at the bare white ceiling.

Again it became still.

Every look was directed at the pale man up there on the pulpit. He spoke with a soft, thin voice, but it sounded full of emotion and verve, it almost seemed as if he was barely holding back the tears himself, "Blessed are the poor in spirit: for theirs is the kingdom of heaven. — Blessed are they that mourn: for they shall be comforted."

He had taken as a basis the words of the Sermon on the Mount, and he pleaded to God who could relieve the distress, to the great almighty God who feeds the birds and clothes the lilies of the field, and the poor people listened to him in dull devotion, and stared at the white folded hands of the man, and outside the rain trickled and swirled, and the blackish mist poured in the door and hindered the breathing of the poorest until the last hymn had been sung and the people had slipped away from there in intractable silence.

The black-haired Hanne stood before the church door, her prayer book under her arm, and next to her stood Klas, sombre and unsettled.

"Did you see, my boy, how she has run after him, to the tavern for a dance?" the old woman muttered, and pointed with gratification down the village street with

her gaunt finger. "Now, was your mother not right? —
Come home, Klas."

She seized him under the arm, and drew him a few
steps with herself.

"Yes, mother," the poor fellow groaned in despair
and walked a stretch of the way with her without however being able to desist from looking around from time
to time.

Then he spoke all sorts of incoherent things about
the dismal times and how it was right to cheer yourself
up a bit. In the tavern there would at least be something
jovial playing, and in the end, he stopped, and looked
questioningly at the old woman.

But the black-haired Hanne knew what that meant,
she was shocked, and walked on as quickly as the mist
and rain would let her.

"Mother — —"

"No, no, Klas."

"Mother, I'll only drink a little schnaps, then we will
go home."

"Klas, let it be, don't take our last few groschen into
the tavern — for such a hussy. Ugh!"

She spat.

He seized the old woman by the arm, and pushed the
bristling woman before himself.

"Mother," he wheezed, "not because of her — we will
stay together — just a glass — that's all."

The old mother begged and moaned and reproached
her son, but Klas pressed forwards, and before the old
woman expected it, a sordid green lantern gleamed before her through the smoky mist, and on the cracked
stone steps of the tavern stood a stocky figure who
grasped one of her hands, and pulled her up with all his
strength.

"Rockabyebaby," gurgled a hoarse voice which the
black-haired Hanne recognised furiously as that of

Jochen Wulkow. "The black-haired Hanne has arrived, my gentle dove; will we dance together again like that time when you gave me a kiss?"

And he pinched her fondly on the arm.

"Old boozer," Hanne whimpered indignantly, and tried to tear herself away once more, only the door of the dance hall had already flown open, and Klas pushed her in fully.

In the long strung-out, white floored room, a large lamp with a green shade hung down from the ceiling. In the corner, behind a brown gallery, sat two musicians. A fiddler and a harpist. The landlord stood in shirtsleeves and green apron behind the counter, and had a great number of potbellied bottles in front of himself, red, yellow, and green. Behind him, a small barrel of beer peered out.

And in this hall, probably twenty couples were dancing.

Each dance lasted quarter of an hour. When it was over, the fellows went to the counter and drank, the girls sat on narrow benches, laughing and pattering with their feet under the table.

And it became later and later, already the hands of the wall clock were pointing to the ninth hour, and still Klas sat with his mother in a corner, and stared into the colourful bustle.

There below, Mieke skipped and whirled past, always in the arms of the gendarme whose spurs cheerfully rattled the beat of the dance.

How she looked at he handsome, sun-tanned man! Her breast flew, her eyes sparkled, her long brown plaits sometimes fluttered about her shoulders and other times entangled about her smug partner as if they wanted to shackle him for eternity to the luscious beauty.

Everyone was looking at this couple, all the girls were envying Mieke.

Never did the gendarme summon a different girl, yes, even when he rested with his partner from dancing, he sat with her at a remote table, and had brought over whatever the landlord had in the kitchen and cellar. His arm slung around her chair, nestled quite close to her, he sat next to her, and twisted his shiny buttons, and played with his sparkling sabre.

It was quite different with Klas, silly Klas, who sat like a dolt next to his old mother and had a ridiculously thick, red head. The gendarme, that was a man who knew how to tell her things about her beauty so that her heart pounded with hidden amazement.

'Miss' he constantly called her, and when he talked about his fiance over there on the mainland, who was a baker's daughter, he sighed every time, and pressed Mieke's hand.

Perhaps he would not yet marry her, and then —

Mieke sprang up — —

Cling, cling, plump, plump, trala!, it rang out from the musician's corner, and the young folk around her began a folk dance.

"Come, Miss, shall we walk through the hall a bit?" the gendarme asked, and offered the girl his arm, "it is getting too hot."

And they walked.

When they came past Klas, Mieke nodded to him, and puckered her mouth with a smile.

"Well, Klas, have you danced with your mother already?" she mocked softly, and when Klas stretched out his gnarled hand to her as if he wanted to hold her back by her brown skirt, she slipped adroitly past him.

The poor fellow groaned.

"Rockabyebaby, my black-haired Hanne," Jochen Wulkow was slurring, already swaying quite drunkenly through the hall, and now sitting down behind the old woman on the window sill. "Will they marry, the green-coat with the sabre. — Do you see, my little hen, you could have too, if you had been her mother. But why didn't you marry your Jochen!"

The black-haired Hanne paid no attention to him. She had almost fallen asleep from weariness, and now patted her son anxiously on his back.

"Now come, Klas, I beg you, I cannot endure it any more. You see though what sort of hussy she is — come, my boy, come."

Klas straightened, sprang up, and with neck bowed forward, he stared madly through the swarm of dancers.

The gendarme and Mieke had just then vanished through a small side door.

Cling, cling, plump, plump, trala!, the music cheered.

"Klas, Klas," the old woman called, only her son no longer heard her.

Without looking left or right, his gaze directed stiffly at the little door, he forced his way through the dancers, mindless of whether he gave this or that couple a powerful push.

What did it have to do with him? Did he just want to see that hussy who had betrayed him, that Mieke who had enticed from his pocket the last groschen, and who was certainly now kissing the gendarme just as she had fondled him a few days before.

Oh that Mieke!

Now he was standing on the flagstones of the hallway from which he could look out onto the country road.

Outside, thick, smoky night had encamped, no stars looked down, only the green lantern, which rocked back and forth creaking on its iron hook, was spreading a bleary light.

But even this bleak light revealed too much for poor Klas.

Did it not flicker about two figures closely nestled together, who were caressing each other, and exchanging sweet words? Did he not see how the man's head bent, how two full arms lifted over his neck, and now — — ?

A growling cry like the bark of a irritated dog sounded. The two moved apart, startled. The next moment, Klas pulled the girl around.

"Come in, Mieke, right now," he wheezed as she sought to escape his damp hand, and the gendarme rattled his spurs, and asked from above, "What do you want, man?"

"Let me go, stupid Klas," Mieke cried hoarsely in the meantime, and ran her nails over his hand, "the gendarme will make a note of you."

"But steady," the policeman strove to affirm himself, and when Klas cried out in fury, and grasped at the girl's arm anew, Mieke's admirer simply shoved him down the steps, and then strode with the loudly laughing girl into the hall.

The sabre rattled behind him, and Klas stood outside in the rain, and shook his fists in impotent jealousy.

Oh that wicked Mieke with the full, soft arms and the red lips; how he hated her, that luscious, beautiful woman, how it ran through him in fervent, wild desire!

He crept up to the illuminated window of the hall, and peered through it.

There she was dancing along again, her head with its curly hair nestled on the chest of the stranger, and the eyes, the eyes —

With a leap, the tormented man stood in the hallway, he went into the hall, rushed up to a round, waiting girl, and threw her around madly in a dance.

"No more — no more!"

Another and yet another, he did not stop; everything turned around him, the walls whirled, the floor swayed, the music screamed like a shrill, raging hunting call!

"Klas!" a despairing voice screamed through the hall.

A gasping, sweat-covered fellow with turbid hair, and and goggling eyes staggered up to black-haired Hanne, and looked at her impatiently.

It was no longer her son, it was a desolate, strange fellow, and an all-conquering horror penetrated the mother, "Klas," she cried and touched him, trembling, "come home, my sweet son, not for my sake, only for yours. God, God, you look like my Jochen when he died."

Only the fellow shook his confused head with coarse laughter.

"No, not right now — now I must show her. Go home alone, mother, I will come after."

"Klas, your old mother ..."

"You are just getting on my nerves here," the poor fellow wheezed in a fury which was otherwise foreign to him, "go instantly, you hear!"

The old woman wanted to keep control of herself, because her neighbours were already whispering and muttering, but after these words, she began sobbing spasmodically, "Klas, if you now — —"

"Go instantly!" the irritated man shouted dark-red with shame, and shot away before Hanne could let her raised arm fall.

Cling, cling, plump, plump, trala!, it cheered around her.

Then the old woman went.

As she strayed out stiffly into the night, into the rain, something crept up unnoticed behind her, a heavy hand suddenly sank down onto the shoulder of the startled woman, and Jochen Wulkow's broken voice said with rough sympathy, "Don't be sad, my black-haired Hanne. To be a parent isn't easy — for see, my Mieke isn't nice to me either, and yet I love her, children are children."

Old Wulkow then stroked his companion's wrinkled cheek.

"With the story there," he concluded quickly, "your late Jochen always occurs to me. For namely to your Jochen, I had once lent a shiny taler, and he wanted to give me a receipt for it; but then I said to him, 'No, Jochen, when you give it back, then it is okay.' And you see, Hanne, it is exactly like that for us with the children's love. When it is given back, then it is okay, and when it is not given back, then it must also be okay."

Mad Johann fell silent, the mist billowed back and forth, and the old woman cried.

The Famine Village

Hanne had barely left the dance hall when the door opened once more, and the gendarme stepped out into the hallway arm in arm with Mieke.

This time the landlord walked in advance of them, and carried a burning candle in his hand. He had asked the gendarme to take a look at the night quarters prepared for him, for the landlord placed some importance on being on the best terms with the green uniformed policeman.

He stopped before a small open room, and shone the candle into it.

The bleak candlelight flickered over a large bed with a massive, red and white flowered cover, as well as over a brown table and a pair of crude chairs.

"It is to your satisfaction?" the polite guide asked with a heavy-handed gesture, and when his celebrated guest assured him after a fleeting glance that 'it is all in order', he withdrew with a broad, smiling grin.

The two were alone.

In the open room, the flame of the candle stump flickered back and forth; outside, the rain trickled over the low window; otherwise, everything was cosy and quiet. And suddenly the gendarme slung his arm around the young woman, and pressed to himself so that her breath skipped.

"You don't fit amongst the farmers, Miss," he erupted stormily as he kissed her, "I love you and swear eternal faith to you — my sweet treasure, aren't you?"

She trembled in his arms; with that he lost control.

With bold violence, he grabbed her and lifted her over the threshold of the room, almost as far as the brown table.

"Do you like me a bit?" he asked, and patted her cheeks lovingly; only Mieke set herself free, and lowered her eyes so that only the long, black eyelashes were visible.

"You have a fiance though over there?" she asked in a strange tone.

"Yes — admittedly."

The gendarme rattled his spurs, and plucked at his beard.

"But I love only you, sweetheart," he continued with a forced laugh. And as if he wanted to divert this conversation, he embraced her anew, and sought her lips stormily.

But this time, Mieke leapt up powerfully, a short struggle took place, then she was free.

Her blood seethed, her bust heaved; for the first time, fervent, wild passion had befallen her.

"It is all just a stupid thing," she burst out with restrained ardour, "for — for won't you want to marry me afterwards??"

It was a question so full of fear, menace and trembling, bewitching covetousness that the handsome man in the green uniform stood helplessly opposite the swaying woman.

One word, one single word, and this beautiful woman over whose cheeks shiver upon shiver chased would be his in blissful desire.

Still he stood and deliberated.

But in the next moment, the military honour was victorious in the former soldier. —

He sighed deeply, and lifted the finger with the narrow gold ring, "Yes, if I did not already have the ring," he murmured distractedly — "and then the circumstances, the tedious money —"

He did not get any further. He just saw a pair of sparkling cat's eyes smouldering before himself, the full arm which he had admired so often rose towards him, and a short, wailing laugh was heard.

Then the place where they had been was empty.

"Devil of a woman," the gendarme murmured, dumbfounded, and threw his sabre furiously into a corner, "why must I tie everything to her straightaway. But the hangman will fetch me if I remain another minute in this hole," he grumbled, and strapped on his sabre again.

"Hey — landlord — hey there!" he shouted loudly out into the corridor. — "Where has the fellow got to?"

In the next moment, the breathless landlord stood before him, and received the instructions to immediately bring the gendarme's horse from the stall.

"What?" the fat man stammered, unable to explain to himself the policeman's sudden change of will. "What? Out into the night now — —"

"Shut up!" the guest commanded, enraged, and when the landlord had vanished, shaking his head, the gendarme strode menacingly up and down before the door to the hall.

Inside the music had fallen silent, a confusion of voices came through indistinctly, and occasionally the clinking of bottles and glasses could be heard. The waiting man thought he heard quite distinctly Mieke's melodious voice, and suddenly he had the handle of the door in his hand, and stepped clattering in.

His sharp eyes sought and found Mieke immediately.

She was sitting over there at the corner table and fingering her plaits upset. Opposite her crouched Klas, his fat head propped in his hands, and his large, aquamarine eyes directed rigidly at the table.

The two seemed to still be sulking with one another.

But a misshapen pedlar was wandering from table to table offering in a broad showcase all sorts of bric-a-brac and objects of jewellery for sale.

"Perhaps a cross for the beautiful young lady?" the little man whispered with a hoarse voice and crept up to Klas's side, "I have bracelets too and coral broaches, pomade, silver earrings, hair-bands, silk shawls; but the most beautiful of all is the cross, made entirely out of large pearls."

"Need nothing," Klas murmured.

Then a hand grasped in the box, and lifted a bracelet up, "How much?" inquired the voice of the gendarme, examining the startled pedlar from head to toe.

The little man threw a timid look about himself, and began stuttering, "For everybody else, a taler," he stammered and bowed deeply before the official, "for the gendarme, however, only ten groschen."

"Here!"

The gendarme threw a coin into the box, and then placed the bracelet of fake coral on the table before Mieke.

"For a souvenir," he said casually as he looked down covetously at her smooth, brown neck, "for eternal memory, Miss."

But the girl did not stir, her head just rose imperceptibly, and looked questioningly over at Klas. And this one look glowed through the poor man like a fervent, intoxicating drink. What strange incitement lay in this look, what teasing familiarity; did it not seem to say, I am fond of you, much fonder that of the puffed-up soldier. Come, Klas, come, don't let him have the last word!

No, and he did not want to leave the green poof this luscious, brown-haired woman — no, no!

He sprang up, glowing red, swallowed the last of the schnaps, and groped hastily in his pocket.

It was empty.

"So take it, Miss!" his enemy urged on the other side, and this time, he dared again to stroke the soft, round arm of Mieke.

Klas rushed away to the bar behind which the landlord stood, and in the next moment, a large silver watch in thick nickel casing lay on the top. —

"Here — for the watch — two talers," the fellow wheezed in a whisper — "it is from my father, quick, Krischan, quick."

The landlord shook his head, grumbled something, and shoved the two talers into the excited fellow's broad, trembling hand.

"The old spendthrift", he grumbled behind him.

But Klas was already standing next to the pedlar, and groping about madly and drunkenly in the box.

"Here the cross," the trader recommended insistently, "genuine Venetian pearls, young gentleman. It is as though made for your fiance, together with the chain it costs only a taler."

No answer, but the taler flew into the box, the hulking fellow with trembling hands placed the chain around his beauty's neck, and the receiver sprang up, and threw herself on his chest in full view.

"How good you are, Klas!" she burst out in a rush, and it seemed as if her words were driven by a secret force, "Now we are fiances. And tomorrow you will give me a ring, won't you?"

"Anything you want, Mieke," Klas stammered in dismay, and the pedlar grinningly fetched two badly gilded brass rings from his trinkets, and buffed them with a leather cloth.

"What does that mean?" the gendarme flared up, having observed the forgoing with barely restrained fury. "What are you doing there?"

The misshapen little man folded up.

"I also have rings for engaged couples," he coughed submissively, and stared helplessly at the policeman. "I am a poor, old man who — —"

"Aha! I thought it," the policeman laughed, "so no trade licence? Well, then no more fuss — forwards, man!"

Clattering, he escorted the wrongdoer to the door; but before he vanished completely, he turned once more, and commanded the landlord imperiously, "The dancing and jiggling must stop. You only have permission until twelve o'clock, take note of that! — Hey, forwards!"

The door fell clanging shut, and soon afterwards the hoofbeats of a trotting horse could be heard.

Sighing, the musicians packed up their instruments, for the poor drops had played for sweet bread, and the disturbed guests went their way ill-temperedly into the village, into misery.

Klas and Mieke were amongst the first to go.

Outside the mist was still billowing, the bleak rain was still trickling down, and settling in thousands of little pearls on the clothes and hair of the walkers. But they both paid no attention. Klas stared rigidly at the pearl cross which rested on Mieke's young, breathing chest, and something rang and sang constantly in Mieke's ear, a sound like the rattling of sabres and clinking spurs.

It infatuated her, made her blood rush, her breath fly, and in blazing desperation, she suddenly embraced her hulking sweetheart, and lifted her hot lips to his ear.

"Klas."

"Mieke, Mieke."

"Do you like me, Klas?" she whispered with wild, contradictory trepidation. He rushed to her, but he did not touch her.

He still stared as though bewitched at the little cross which rose and fell quicker and quicker, quicker and quicker. — If the gendarme had not yet left his hard head, did the warning image of his old mother arise before him once more?

But as if the shuddering girl had guessed it, she whispered contritely, "I just wanted to make you jealous. Come, Klas, be good to me again."

They stood now before Jochen Wulkow's old dilapidated clay shack. Everything was dark, nothing stirred within.

"Is he asleep already?" Klas asked, breathing heavily, and Mieke shook her head, and answered in a whisper, "Eh, Sunday evenings he always runs over to Rohrdorf, and only comes back towards morning. — Well, good night, Klas."

She slowly stretched her warm hand out to him, and looked to him with her peculiar, luminous eyes.

Then it happened to him.

The rain was swishing down all around, smoky haze skimmed before the wind, and the cracked roof of the dilapidated smoke house hid two young, lost humans.

Georg Engel

It was early in the morning. The moon still stood behind the leaden-grey clouds, and its bleak light
reflected strangely on the large puddles on the village
street.

Deep below, where the eternally moving sea usually
stretched out, an uncanny, unyielding, impenetrable
nothing was encamped. Sky, water and the nearby green
coast, it was all blackish, indistinct haze, a motionless,
horrible nothing.

About this time, the black-haired Hanne strode out
from her little house, and approached a small half-rotted wooden pump from which the villagers ladled
drinking water.

And the mist swirled so thickly around her that the
old woman did not notice at all the other female figure
who already seemed to expect her arrival at the pump.
Only when Hanne had hung her bucket on the iron bar
did her gaze fall on the poor young woman entirely
draped in rags, and she nodded to her wordlessly.

The other woman also remained silent, and only
when the bucket was filled did she help Hanne with tak-
ing it down, and then remained standing before her,
"Hanne, I have a request for you."

The old woman shook her head a little. "What is it
then, Liese?" she murmured downcast.

"Will you lend me a little milk," the younger woman
asked, "it is for the little one, otherwise the child is a
goner, the poor worm. I don't have a single piece of

bread in the house, and my man has been lying for three weeks now."

The pale, emaciated woman passed her hand over her eyes and cried.

The old woman lifted up the bucket, "The poor, poor Jöhr," she said sympathetically, "but I myself don't have a drop. It is too awful now."

With that she wanted to huff and puff away with her heavy load, only the desperate young mother held her back by the skirt.

"Then lend me money," she cried, "just a few pfennigs!"

But again the old woman shook her head and stared up into the mist, "I don't have a pfennig," she murmured dully, "where should I take one from now, it is all used up."

"So, all of it?" the poor woman gnashed now with an outburst of scorn. "And your Klas throws around the talers?"

"What?" the black-haired Hanne asked, remaining rooted to the spot.

"And buys such a hussy the most expensive jewellery?" the other continued with a triumphant laugh. "Well, but he got his beating."

Now it was too much for Hanne though, and when even more village women arrived, and made all sorts of mocking comments to her, she rose her hand dismissively and, deeply injured in her maternal love, she brought forth the words, "That is all gossip; you merely envy me my Klas because he has been so good to me up to now."

But the doubt and the yearning to be able to understand the strange talk of the village women rang through her faith, and as she lingered for a moment, the women all shouted and mocked and laughed dizzyingly.

"Didn't you hear the racket last night?" wailed the first woman.

"And how Jochen Wulkow blustered when he found his house locked, and inside — well, ha ha!"

"And how Mieke sprang to the window, and don't you know what from?" a third continued as she rolled her eyes from shame or delight, "and how your dear son wanted to beat up old Mad Johann as well?"

Thus it continued for quite a while yet, and Hanne stood, and listened to every word, every single word, which cut her to the heart until she suddenly gathered up her bucket, and said quite calmly, "Thank you, it is okay; such a thing is not so bad with bride and groom — adieu."

Her heart was breaking as she said it, two big tears were rolling over her gaunt cheeks, but she carried the bucket to her shack without stopping once.

The women at the pump though looked at her perplexed, and did not know whether they should trust their ears.

"Yes, if it is so," rasped the same woman who had berated the most before, "then it really is — — — look at one, bride and groom," she continued without connection; "there you can see again what a boozer our Mad Johann is, can't you?"

"Yes," the others agreed. "A disgraceful fellow."

***

When the black-haired Hanne stepped into her little home, it was still all dark within.

Klas lay in deep slumber in the adjoining room, and the old woman listened to his heavy breathing through the cracks in the door.

But strangely, today the indistinct noise was transformed for the mother into all sorts of words and sounds, into cries of yearning and pet names which did not refer to her, but to the younger, the more loved woman.

That was not to be changed anymore.

Shrugging her shoulders, she lit a small tallow candle, and crept with it into that corner where the red moiré birch-wood commode stood which she had brought with her as a young girl into her marriage with Jochen. And there he hung himself, her dear, good Jochen, right above the commode, and although it was only a blurred, long faded slide, it seemed to Hanne though as if those grey eyes came to life, as if the broad, bearded mouth really spoke to her. She held the candle stump quite close to the little picture, and removed a speck of dust from the round glass with her forefinger.

But then she began to commune with the picture of her blessed man, and poured out her entire heart to it.

"My poor Jochen," she murmured, "when you took leave of me that night, I promised you that our Klas would become an upright man. And you are now up above, Jochen, and know all that I have done to that end. He is a kindhearted boy too, but see, husband, there is now such a thing happening in him, and he cannot act any differently. Mieke is a pretty girl too, much saucier that I was when you gifted me the beautiful soap heart, and isn't it true, Jochen, that you must close one eye when everything is not like it should be? But it will all be good. Pray rightly with our dear God for our Klas, and when you can, Jochen, then fetch me soon. For see, you must put up with me, but if the boy then comes — — — Oh, husband, husband, all that you have slumbered through."

She stared at the picture for a moment longer, then she extinguished the candle, and walked slowly, but decisively, into the adjoining room.

There Klas lay on his straw mattress, and was looking around with tired eyes.

He had already woken long before, and now lay there with aching head and pounding heart thinking again and ever again about the beautiful woman who had been his and whom he would never give up again.

Then the door creaked, a shuffling step was heard, and a gentle cough, and suddenly the recumbent man stretched out, and pressed his head deep into the pillow. His mother was coming, his old mother, and something like hot, torturous shame stirred in him, an inexplicable fear rose in him of looking today into that gaunt, wrinkled countenance.

He lay motionless, and appeared fast asleep.

Only the old woman did not leave.

She gently placed her trembling hand on his head, and when Klas now looked up timidly, his mother spoke earnestly and solemnly, "Get up, Klas, and fetch your bride. I want to marry you, and bless you; and your father above will pray for you."

Her voice sounded weak and gentle, her hand trembled on his hair, and Klas covered his eyes, and sobbed in wild, inexplicable woe, "Mother — mother!"

The Famine Village

It had turned spring. Countless, luminous white clouds chased across the sky, and threw their fleeting, scurrying shadows onto the sunlit village street. Glistening, filmy water dripped down from the trees and bushes, and below the spraying, stormy sea thundered and roared.

A yellow brimstone butterfly was fluttering in the tepid air. —

It had turned spring, spring, and the tired, desperate eyes of the pinched fishermen rose longingly towards the new, mild light; perhaps, it would bring crops, perhaps the hard earth would finally, finally burst and let the golden seeds shoot up which would make them bread, the precious bread.

What a winter had passed by them!

In the deep snow, almost buried in their shacks; frost, hunger and illness within; and no work and the deathly, creeping boredom.

Now Klas knew what it meant to feed a family.

Since Mieke, the beautiful, luscious, brown-haired wife, had taken command in the black-haired Hanne's house, the worries had moved in with him.

What had not sufficed for two, was never enough for three anymore; he had to fetch, acquire, earn, Mieke had said to him — but how, how?

And then Mieke. —

He loved her so much, this slender full busted woman. An affectionate look from her luminous eyes still sufficed to make him stand for minutes before her, and when he admired in silent delight her rounded, soft shoulders, her full arms, and her long, gleaming hair, he could then forget instantly that shortly before contention and discord had reigned in the small house.

He considered them small frictions, but it was hate, smouldering, hidden, growing hate which daily struck new roots in the young woman's heart against Klas's old mother.

The old woman snooped about her, the old woman gossiped about her with the other villagers, the old woman ate the best pieces, the old woman grudged her every enjoyment, incited stupid, fatuous Klas against her, the stupid fool whom she had married in order to be free, free like the yellow butterfly out there. The old woman counted out every groschen for her, the old woman hauled and drudged all day long only so that the others saw what a lazy, unemployable thing her unwished for daughter was, the old woman, the old woman, oh that hateful old woman ruined the air for breathing. She had to go away, away, all the same whether defeated or dead; and yet —

It had turned spring.

In the little shack, Mieke sat at the window, and plaited her long, nut brown hair. Before her on the window latch hung a small, rectangular mirror, and when the young woman bent her arms back behind her head, when the wide sleeves of her pink flowered calico jacket fell back, and a piece of gleaming brown skin was exposed, then the mirror showed the woman in her beguiling, victorious, dangerous beauty.

It was just as she was raising one plait over her shoulder and putting a colourful little ribbon around the end that outside a groan was heard, and at the same time, the window darkened.

On the village street, the black-haired Hanne was shuffling along, and hauling on her back a large basket under whose load the old woman was moaning and groaning. The drops of sweat were running from her heated forehead, her worn-out feet did not seem to want to carry the old woman any further.

"Mieke, Mieke!" she burst out, struggling for breath, and when the named woman did not appear straight-away on the threshold, Hanne complained once more with the impatience of age, "Mieke, I can't go on."

Klas's wife threw the plait back over her shoulder, and rose reluctantly from her chair.

The old woman always had to disturb her, always just when she least expected it.

Without particular haste, she walked outside, and placed herself opposite the exhausted woman without a greeting.

"What's up?" she asked curtly.

"Take the basket of sticks off me," Hanne whimpered tearfully, "oh my shoulders, how it cuts — I must rub myself with paraffin."

And as Hanne propped herself on the wall of the little house with her outstretched arm, Mieke lifted the basket with youthful strength from the ground, "Nothing at all," she then suggested nonchalantly, and strode after the mother into the living room. "But you surely went the longest way again?"

The black-haired Hanne nodded, "Straight through the village," she wheezed, and pulled her woolen jacket off. "It is less damp there now."

Hardly had the mother emitted this that the young woman turned blood-red, and flung the full basket with a jolt into the corner.

"Straight through the village," she repeated with erupting fury, "so that all can see and commiserate with you — well? But you always act like that," she laughed loudly, and walked up and down the room with short steps, "but I would do it differently," she murmured in a way barely still comprehensible, "either way."

Meanwhile the black-haired Hanne had sat down at the table, and was rubbing her exposed shoulder on which a broad, red streak was visible.

At the same time, she paid no attention at all to the talk of her new daughter. She seemed to be used to such talk, yes, after some time, she even asked quite amiably, "Where is the paraffin then, my daughter?"

"I don't know," Mieke threw over her shoulder at her.

"But it stood on your cupboard."

The young woman continued her quick, defiant pacing. "Then I poured the thing out," she said with indifference, "it lies on the rubbish heap perhaps."

The old woman suddenly began to tremble, and grasped at the table top spasmodically in her agitation. The creases in her face became deeper, her eyes receded, and her nose seemed pointed and hook-like. She looked unlovely as she now burst out with a very high voice, "Klas must know that, and as soon as he comes home, I will tell him. No, no, don't look at me like that, Klas must inform you that you don't push around his mother like that; this time I'll certainly tell him."

"A thousand times for my sake," Mieke laughed snappishly.

She paused in the middle of the room as she said it, and looked steadily at the old woman.

It was a look as long and strange as if she had just fastened on a strong, irrevocable decision. Then, trilling a little song, she strode out into the courtyard, and left the enraged Hanne alone.

A few pieces of white washing were hung out to dry over the house's green mossy fence, and next to them, grey, red and blue woolen cloths moved back and forth in the fresh breeze.

Mieke went to this place and placed both hands on two free points of the fence. She actually wanted to take down the fluttering, sun-dried linen pieces, but when the young woman rocked back and forth slowly in the mild, warm air, when the spring wind skimming past made her cheeks shiver with its cool breath, it overcame her like a numbing, dreamy intuition.

Lost in thought, she continued rocking; she did not know herself anymore.

Then vague hoofbeats clattered up the village street, something flashed and sparkled in the sunlight, a peaked helmet became visible, a handsome, green uniformed rider, and now Mieke lifted her head, and placed her hand before her eyes, peering out.

Her heart was pounding vigorously, her hands were trembling, the rider pulled up directly at her house.

Old thoughts rose in her, the young woman fell for the sun's magic.

A bright whinnying interrupted her, and at the same time, the gendarme sprang from the horse, and placed two fingers to his helmet in a military salute.

A short blond full beard now framed his tanned countenance, and made him appear even more handsome than before. He stood quite close before Mieke, only the fence separated the two. "I have an order to talk to you," the official began somewhat bashfully, and twisted his moustache. "Does your husband's mother still live with you?"

"Yes."

"How old is she?" the gendarme asked, and wrote Mieke's information down with great importance into a thick notebook.

Then he inquired at length about Hanne's religion, when she had become a widow, whether she was often ill, and how large Klas's income was, and made the young woman so confused by this mysterious investigation that she finally placed her finger to her lips, and asked curiously what it all meant.

"I don't know," the gendarme answered, shoving the book carefully again into his tunic. "I have received the orders from the County Commissioner and can't give any more information."

With that he wanted to mount his horse again, but he hesitated half way, and looked around in bewilderment.

Mieke was standing before him and smiling. She had placed both hands over a fence paling, the sunlight was throwing a glittering pollen onto the tips of her hair, she seemed to him even more supple, even more beautiful than a year before.

"Well?" she asked softly as if she was out of breath, "married already?"

"No."

He remained rooted to the spot, and blinked at her with bashful admiration.

Since she was the wife of another, his martial honour prescribed some timidity towards her, and yet — a vague feeling held him back.

"No, I am still not married," he continued without thinking, "my fiance is ill. — In eight to ten weeks perhaps."

"So, so," Mieke murmured with a peculiar tone of voice, "that is nice," and when the young man made a gesture of farewell, she slowly stretched out her hand over the fence to him.

It was a soft, warm hand, and when the young man touched it reluctantly, a strange, trembling complacency streamed through him.

"Can you not tell me what it has to do with my mother?" Mieke coaxed, and leant even further over the fence.

His hand still rested in hers, and he responded uncertainly, "This afternoon perhaps, if it is possible for
me."

"Yes, this afternoon, I would really like to know."

"Well, then I will call on you once more. — Adieu."

With a leap, he again sat on his steed, and rode away
in a trot from there.

His helmet flashed in the morning sun, his sabre
banged incessantly against the well-fed animal, and
Mieke sent a long, inquisitive look after him.

When she stepped back into the house, she was smiling again.

Towards midday, Klas returned from the sea in his large waterproof boots, and then threw a few damp, strong smelling nets wordlessly in a corner.

"Nothing again?" the old woman inquired anxiously as Mieke leant by the window in silence.

Klas sat on the bench by the oven, and laboriously pulled his boots off.

"No," he said sombrely after a while, "we fished for salmon, but they aren't coming up this year, not a single one — I soon won't know what to do anymore."

An anxious silence occurred, nobody dared break it.

Then Klas lifted his hulking head, and looked at his wife who was looking out steadily at the bright village street. Instinctively he sighed deeply, and brushed the green tiles of the oven in despair. — — —

Nobody had such a slender, desirable wife as he; she could have been so happy with him — then the hardship moved in, and did not let it come to any proper love.

"Mieke," Klas cried in a low voice to himself, "you have not yet given me your hand."

"Well, she probably knows why too," the black-haired Hanne grumbled, having placed a few earthen bowls on the table for the meagre midday meal. "She was so bad to me again, Klas, and at the same time, I am an ill woman now who can't work anymore."

That too now —

Klas scratched behind his air grumpily, and crept in his socks over to his wife.

"You should get along, Mieke," he murmured affectionately, "mother means well with you."

He wanted to place his arm around her shoulders at the same time, but Mieke turned away vehemently, and pushed his hand back.

"Go to your mother," she then said quite calmly, "she has earned it too."

Oh, she knew how this cool calm worked on the stupid Klas!

"See, Klas, she acts like that," black-haired Hanne now erupted in her agitation from the other side, and sought seeking help with her lively grey eyes those of her son. Only Klas had been watching his beautiful, young wife the entire time, and now growled irritatedly at the old woman, "You have done something too though, leave me in peace."

With that he walked into the adjoining room with long strides, threw the door shut behind him, and sought for a conspicuously long time for a pair of old wooden clogs. When he entered again, the two women were already sitting at the table before a bowl of mashed potatoes, and Klas noticed that his mother had a red, tearful countenance.

He felt sorry again, and when he had sat down next to her, he asked her quite amiably, "Well, mother, is there something good?"

The old woman overcame herself, and looked at her son sorrowfully. All the suppressed pain stamped itself on her features.

"What shall there be now?" she murmured brokenly — "potatoes, they won't last. And for you, Klas, still a piece of grilled bacon."

At the same time, she shoved the crisp piece across to him, and although Klas breathed in the strong smell eagerly, he said, following a sudden flush, "Give it to Mieke, she likes it so much too."

Only that went down badly with the black-haired Hanne. "No, no," she cried incautiously, "it was made for you, Klas; — you have the hard work, you alone and not — — —"

The old woman did not finish her sentence, for Mieke rose suddenly, and went silently to the water bucket to ladle a fresh drink.

Klas looked around anxiously at her, then he threw an irritated glance at his mother, and finally cut the piece of bacon in three equal pieces.

"So," he murmured awkwardly, when Mieke had returned to her place, and placed each piece in the bowl. "Now we will all taste it, won't we, Mieke?"

But the two woman did not touch the dish, and the poor fellow also choked down his piece with simulated hunger.

It again went silent, the three did not speak with each other anymore.

Only when the old woman was clearing away the dishes did Mieke step behind her husband's seat and place her hand on his shoulder, "You will go over to Rohrdorf to ask at the salt makers whether they could use you?" she suggested insistently. "You will go, won't you?"

"Come with me," Klas asked, springing up.

"No, no, I have things to do here this afternoon."

"Well, as you wish, Mieke," Klas acceded, and patted her lovingly on the arm. "You are right."

He got ready to go, said goodbye and set off. When he turned around once more on the village street, he saw Mieke standing at the window and nodding to him. Behind her, already in the shade of the sagging roof, stood his old mother, and it seemed as if she was folding her hands devoutly over her breast.

Perhaps the old woman was praying for him, perhaps he was finally, finally going towards his fortune. — —

Before Mieke's former home, the miserable, dilapidated smoke house, he met his father-in-law, Jochen Wulkow, who was crouching comfortably on the threshold and blowing massive clouds of smoke from a short pipe towards the sun.

"How goes it?" Klas asked.

"Good."

"Why?"

"Well why?" Jochen repeated, and opened his half-closed eyes, "I have made an invention."

"That's not possible," his son-in-law suggested in amazement.

"Yes, I can especially now dream what I want," the old man countered quite calmly. — "Once I dreamt of the finest food, then I dreamt of a sack of gold, and then I imagined that I threw the landlord out of his tavern because he could not pay me — — — Can you lend me a six?" he continued his explanation serenely.

"No," Klas said pityingly.

"Well, then adieu," Jochen nodded, blinking into the sun again, "have a good trip."

With long strides, Klas hurried on, to the goal, to his fortune.

He already had almost an hour of walking behind him, the sun was already beginning to redden and float in delicate veils of mist, when a fast rider galloped towards him, and Klas recognised without difficulty the gendarme who rode past him arrogantly.

In short time, the hoofbeats were fading away.

"Well, all the same," Klas thought cheerfully, "I married Mieke nicely out from under his nose."

By the ditch of the main road, a daisy was flowering. The walker plucked it, and stuck it on his hat, he felt so daring.

Georg Engel

Three hours later, Klas crept back the same way. It had become evening, the stars stood in the sky, and from the sea, a cold wind was rising.

The poor fellow hardly noticed. Fury and rage were fermenting in him.

It was all in vain again. The salt maker in Rohrdorf had already released a portion of his workers days before, and had only a regretful shrug of the shoulders for Klas. The sweat broke out on the strong fellow when he imagined how he would have to share the news of misfortune with the two women. And then a wild fear befell him, that his young wife was tiring of this mournful life, that she could turn away from him, and that he would then be miserable beyond all measure. And this depressing feeling in his chest became so overpowering that he could have groaned out loud.

"Forward, forward," he said encouragingly to himself. "There is only half an hour to go!"

Wheezing, he stormed onward through the night. And again hoofbeats sounded to his side, and when he turned around in surprise, a dark riding figure tore along the whispering poplars of the main road, a hulking figure hung almost over the animal's neck, and clop, clop it went into the darkness.

Klas began to shiver, but he pulled himself together once more.

"It is all nonsense," he murmured with chattering teeth, and ran forwards in mad haste, "home, home!"

In a few minutes, he had put the long stretch behind him, and soon stood breathless before his little house.

Thank God, it was all still; a weak candlelight penetrated through the window of the room in which he and Mieke slept; and when he approached, he saw through a crack in the wooden casement his wife lying dressed on the bed, her head buried deep in the pillows so that you could only discern her back.

Klas's heart pounded.

The poor thing had surely been waiting a long time for him, and she must surely have been overtaken by sleep. With a leap, the alarmed man stood in the small living room, so that the black-haired Hanne, sitting hunched by the hearth, emitted a loud cry, and he threw his hat carelessly on the table.

But why did his mother not ask him at all about the result of his journey, why was she crouching there by the cold hearth and shivering incessantly?

"Has something happened to Mieke?" Klas cried suddenly in nameless, shaking fear, and propped himself staggering against the table — "Mother, is she — —"

The old woman started. Her eyes were glassy, her tongue seemed paralysed in her open, trembling mouth. But then she burst out quickly and incoherently, "What should she be? — No, no, my son, I know nothing — it is all okay, all okay — all okay."

Her hands groped about convulsively on the hearth, she only gradually seemed to calm down.

"Mieke!" Klas cried and sprang over to the doorway of the room from where he could discern his stretched out wife. "Has something happened?"

She straightened up, and looked at him with an uncertain smile.

Two bright, red spots glowed on her cheeks.

"You surely went in vain?" she asked as her lips trembled strangely.

"Entirely in vain, entirely in vain — but here, what has happened here?"

"Has your mother not told you? — So, I thought; now then — the gendarme was here."

Her voice swelled somewhat stronger, and at the same time, she sprang down completely from the bed. In the living room, Hanne was meanwhile walking up and down, and murmuring, and outside a brief wind gust blew against the shack.

Klas inclined his hulking head towards his wife, and let his gaze stray erratically into the corners.

"The gendarme?" he murmured dully, "Here — with you two — with you — Mieke?"

"Well, why not then? He had an order to go to us."

From inside where the black-haired Hanne was walking up and down, a fearful, sharp noise sounded in between, as if the old woman was coughing or laughing.

Klas paid no attention, but repeated it, as it were, as if he had awoken from a difficult dream, "An order? — —"

She stood ingenuously opposite him now, and was adroitly binding the woolen shawl tighter which he had torn down in his agitation.

"What sort of orders?" the returning man wheezed, shaking his wife off anew.

"He came because of mother."

Inside the old woman laughed again.

"Mieke?"

"Well?"

"What was it?"

Mieke became impatient, bit her lip, and clenched her hands together.

"Now that's enough," she cried finally with a shaking, hoarse voice, and turned her back to her husband scornfully. "Brings not a pfennig home, and does not want to permit that another brings something good into his house."

"Will you finally tell me?" Klas called, restraining himself, and in the same moment, Mieke became quite serious again, and told him with her mellifluous voice, "Think, Klas, it is great luck in our current circumstances. The gendarme in fact brought a letter from the County Commissioner, and it states within that your mother, if she wants, can be taken immediately into a retirement home in the city. Our Pastor made a submission because of the great misery, and then three people from our village were chosen. My father is also among them. Aren't you pleased that we are finally free of the great worry? I though it would be so nice if I could tell you."

She now stood next to him, and gently touched his arm. And suddenly her husband started, shook himself, and drew her fiercely to himself.

The soft, warm feminine lips seemed to infuse him with new life, "It is great fortune," he stuttered still half apprehensive, and turned to the living room. "Mother, it is great fortune."

The old woman did not answer. She stood at the hearth, and wiped her hands back and forth incessantly.

"You will have it much better there," her son continued, still holding his young wife in his arms.

"And a quite different care," Mieke added.

"Yes, and no work, and calm."

"Let me stay with you, Klas," a hoarse, imploring voice sobbed, and Hanne turned, and stretched both hands towards her son. But as if he had not understood her, Klas stared at the old woman without paying any heed that Mieke had secretly prodded him in the side.

"Don't send me away, my sweet son," his mother murmured, and sat down impotently on a chair, "I want to do everything for you, even more than before. You don't know — — you don't know — — —"

Mieke stirred, "Now, am I right?" she whispered as her eyes began to sparkle peculiarly.

"Shut up," the old woman squawked and looked at the young woman so that she winced, "shut up — you are guilty of everything, you bad, bad — —"

She sought after an expression, but sank down again before she found it.

Mieke had turned pale as snow, and was breathing heavily. "And you stand for such a thing?" she asked in a low voice, and shook the arm of her husband.

"Quiet!" Klas insisted, straightening up forcibly, and placed his large hand on his mother's head. "Mother, you must consider it calmly, for you see — —"

"Oh, my son, you don't know — I cannot tell you why, but it is necessary that I stay here."

He caressed her white hair spasmodically.

"You would take a great worry from me," he groaned in torturous agony, "I don't know anymore where I shall get things from, and hence — — — Did the gendarme make you so afraid of the retirement home?"

A suppressed scream suddenly shrilled through the room. Furious, with hair falling down, Mieke sprang before the struggling man, and tore him around in wild fear, "Don't listen to her," she burst out with trembling lips, "she just wants to put herself between us."

Hanne lifted her head again, and let her grey eyes rest penetratingly on the shaking young woman. Then she nodded several times, and answered calmly, "I did not speak to the gendarme."

Those few words penetrated the hulking fellow like an icy knife without him knowing why.

"Mother, you didn't — — why did he not come to you then?"

The old woman swallowed for a moment, then she said with the same stiff, despondent calm, "Mieke had given me the washing. I was down at the beach, and washing."

It went quiet.

The candle stump in the pewter holder on the stove threw its bleak, yellow glow onto a twitching, pale grey, man's countenance.

"Mieke," he murmured, "Mieke —"

Then he rose, his wife backed away up to the bedroom, her wide-open, greenish-brown eyes always directed firmly at him. By the doorway, however, she clasped the door, and remained standing defiantly before him.

"Strike me," she burst out with fluttering breast, and bent forward as if she had already received the blow. "She has again really got you this far with your stupid jealousy. — Strike me, but I tell you — if your mother does not go, then I will go, and even if I must beg."

"Ugh," Hanne screamed wailing, "dear God, help a poor, old woman!"

The young woman in the doorway had thrown her hand forward accusingly as if she wanted to depict the expanses into which she would go. At the same time, a piece of her full, gleaming arm was exposed, her youthfully strong body shook, her eyes flashed.

"Mieke," Klas stammered, and sank onto her chest, "do you — love me?"

She kissed him, and drew him through the doorway. Then the light was extinguished in the room.

The black-haired Hanne, however, sat by the hearth, and sobbed bitterly.

Georg Engel

Two hours later, in the middle of the night, Klas again crept into the living room, and paused when he found his mother still sitting by the hearth.

The candle stump was flickering back and forth. It had almost burnt down.

"I could not sleep," Klas murmured apologetically, and leant by the hearth. "The wind howls so much."

In fact, it was storming and raging outside so that the wind penetrated through all the cracks in the shack and made the residents shiver.

The spring storms were sweeping over the land.

"Mother — you must go," Klas stuttered uncertainly after a short pause. — "After what has happened here — — —"

He did not dare to express it and scraped with his thick finger about the candle.

"My son, my poor son," the old woman sighed, and shrugged her gaunt shoulders as if she had been thinking something else altogether.

The candle's little flame flickered to and fro fearfully before the air streaming in.

"She wants it absolutely," Klas continued with visible overcoming, and pressed his fist against his forehead. "She does not want to live together with you anymore, not for an hour, the hardship is also too great, and if she leaves me, then, mother, then — —"

The big, hulking man sobbed suddenly, an inaudible, inner sobbing which made the giant figure shake.

And this sobbing the mother could not endure.

The old head and hands began to tremble, then she brushed her apron down, and asked with a dry, broken voice, "Klas — must — must I go?"

No answer.

"And you love your wife surely more than me?"

He remained silent, and did not take his large hands away from his face.

"Klas, must I go?" Hanne cried once more in her heart's fear, and opened her grey eyes wide.

"Yes — mother — it is for the best — you will have it quite different there too — and the young belong together, Mieke — perhaps —"

Again he fell silent, and turned his face in inner shame away from the old woman. But the latter slowly rose, and nodded her head several times, "Beautiful, beautiful," she said hastily, "then I will surely have to go. It must surely be so. — Beautiful, beautiful."

Trembling, she pulled her shawl closer, and walked quickly to the table. There she paused, and embraced her son once more with a single fearful, extremely pained look.

"Why are you looking at me so, mother?"

"Klas, oh, you don't know, I cannot say —"

"You — can—not — tell me —?"

"I wanted to keep you away from it — my poor, poor child; but if it is so — no, I know nothing."

Klas became deathly pale, fumbled with both hands on the hearth, and stared at his mother with streaming eyes.

"What can't you say?" he gurgled, pushing each word out individually, "do you know something about my — about Mieke?" — —

It sounded so disconsolate that his mother was drawn inexorably to him. And suddenly she shuffled up to him, and drew his head to her breast.

"Klas," her hoarse voice intoned, "perhaps it is better thus — I am your mother, and must tell you whom you can be fond of and whom not. Yes, I want to tell you too," she continued amidst tears, since Klas did not stir; "she does not deserve it — oh, Klas, if you had seen —"

"What, what?"

"My poor child; as I returned from the sea — in your own room — — with the gendarme — no, no, control yourself, my son."

A derisive laugh rang out behind them.

Mieke was standing in the doorway of the bedroom, and stretching her bare arm out menacingly towards the old woman. The fear which filled her had not let her rest, it made every fibre in her shake, it was depicted in her distorted face, and it rang out from the cry which screamed from her dry lips. It was an inexplicable, raging, mad fear which screamed from her.

"All lies, Klas, don't believe her — she just wants to separate us — — I love you, Klas, I love you."

She wanted to rush up to him as she was, but then, then —

Was it the provocative voice, was it the overpowering fury? With a short, bull-like roar, the poor man tore himself from the arms of the old woman, it jerked before his eyes, a hot stream shot roaring through his throat, he sprang at his wife, seized her, and buried his fingers roaring into her bare shoulders.

She swayed, she screamed, her entire body crumpled, and with deadly hate in her eyes, she clasped with both hands the fist falling down on her.

"Lies," she implored once more, and pulled herself trembling to him. "Strike me dead — but it is lies —" she whispered once more, and leant her head against his chest. "Don't believe her, Klas, don't believe her — you will be sorry."

Her trembling hands lead his to her mouth.

"So you trust the cheeky hussy more than your mother?" the old woman now screamed in flaring indignation, and tore with crooked fingers at her skirt, "then you are worthy of her and I will go at once."

Mieke looked up at him, her lips stammered something, he distinctly felt her heart pounding against his own, and suddenly a deep, whistling breath, a dull roar and a short, gurgling cry.

"So a pack of lies?" it poured from her lips as he rushed to the old woman.

"Klas, I, your mother — — she's — the gendarme —"

Only the old woman was unable to complete her sentence; it all burnt in him, he emitted a short, hoarse sound, and with outstretched arm, he lunged at the swaying old woman.

***

"Klas!" Mieke screamed appalled, and endeavoured to touch his arm with concealed horror.

The first thing Klas perceived again was the candle stump on the hearth. He was himself crouching on the stone floor, and had in his hands the old woman's head, which lay stiff and motionless between his knees.

Thick black drops, though, were forcing their way through her white hair.

The flame of the candle stump flickered as fearfully as if it wanted to lend the pale countenance the appearance of life once more, but it remained hard, implacably stiff, and Klas stared with deep hanging lower lip and mad, lacklustre gaze at the deeply shrunken, closed eyes.

He sat there motionless, only when one of the dark drops of blood ran over his fingers did he shake his head in insensible numbness.

"Klas," the young woman whispered once more, hoarse with fear, but without stirring from her place, "listen, I can't endure it anymore."

Since that moment when the man foaming in fury had flung his mother from himself, and the old woman had collapsed soundlessly on the sharp edge of the table, since that time, Mieke had stood with stooped body over her husband, and had not dared to break the fearful silence by the lightest of movements.

"Klas — answer me — is she dead?"

He did not stir, and stared incessantly at the stiff countenance as if he were seeing it then for the first time.

Something mad, insensible lay in this collapsed male figure, and Mieke began to shake all over.

"I cannot look anymore," she burst out shuddering, "don't sit like that there — Klas, take her away so that she won't be found here; Klas, Klas, aren't you listening, you should say something!"

"Mother," Klas murmured, and nodded several times with a heavy head, "mother."

A wind gust rattled the windowpanes, and in the same moment, the young woman emitted a piercing scream.

"Just not that anymore — just not that anymore."

The dull-witted, nodding man at her feet, the white-haired body, and the twitching, racing heart in the breast — she was not able to endure it anymore.

Feverish heat, a chill and at the same time a frenzied fear were shaking her body, and dressed in only a shirt and a woolen skirt, she sprang to the door, and stormed out into the night in bare feet.

In the half-dark space, however, the abandoned man still sat and nodded, and murmured to himself.

Meanwhile his wife was running as though chased through the still village lane, always against the roaring wind.

She did not stop until just before the door to Jochen Wulkow's old smokehouse. Now she knew what she intended, why she had hurried here. She must have someone about her, a being who could talk, bluster, curse her, just not be alone with the silent, nodding man.

A gentle push opened the rotten door of the shack, the young woman forced her way into the raven-black room, and tore the snoring old man from his heap of seaweed.

"What?" Jochen Wulkow rasped drowsily, "what?"

"It's me — Mieke — father, I —"

"What — what do you want, Mieke?"

She threw herself down on him, screamed, and whispered something, and sprang up again.

"What? what?" the old man asked with concern, not having grasped the meaning of the confused words.

No answer.

The young woman had long before hurried to the door again, and vanished into the darkness.

"Something isn't right," Jochen murmured in bewilderment, and since he usually camped clothed on his seaweed litter, he rose hurriedly, and limped without any ado after his daughter.

"Nothing will have happened to my Hanne?" he thought along the way as he pulled his open jacket tight about himself.

After a few seconds, he was already standing before Klas's little house, but found the door firmly bolted, and only after repeated pounding was it cautiously opened for him by Mieke.

Mad Johann had done lively justice to the bottle that evening. But the sight which was now presented to him took the intoxication away from him, and left him paralysed.

To begin with, he remained standing calmly on the threshold, and wiped away with his hand two large tears which were running down his cheeks, but then he wailed loudly, threw himself down next to the old woman, suddenly sprang up, and shook Klas by the arm; but the crouching man did not seem to notice his presence at all, and only when the intruder made an effort to lift the stretched out figure from the floor did Klas shake his head with a dull grumbling.

"Let father," Mieke cried, wrestling with her husband's hands imploringly, "he shall take her away so that she isn't found here."

Again the same dull sound, like the furious growl of a predator from whom you want to tear away the prey.

"What?" the old man cried in response as he looked mournfully into Klas's countenance, "I should leave her to you, the one who killed my Hanne? Ugh, God preserve me — your mother, your own mother. — But she still lives, she must come to — she cannot be dead yet!" he burst out vehemently, and cushioned the stiff figure gently in his arms, "and I don't want to have anything more to do with you, you — you murderer."

That was his last word.

Then he slowly carried his burden out the door. As long as he was still lingering on the threshold, Klas remained sitting dully and impassively, but the door had hardly fallen shut behind Jochen when he rose ponderously, looked first in bewilderment at Mieke, who was leaning by the window, shivering, then at the empty place where his old mother had lain until then, and suddenly he broke out into a bloodcurdling howl, and staggered after the old man, sobbing loudly.

The night air brought him to his senses, it tore through the grey mist which had lain over his mind un til then, and with icy clarity, his deed came before his eyes.

That white hair — those drops of blood. —

He screamed so that it echoed far over the dunes and sea, and struck his giant fists loudly against his forehead.

Jochen Wulkow's shack was firmly locked, and although Klas pushed against it with hands and feet, it did not open for him.

"Jochen," the unfortunate man begged imploringly, "just to see her once more."

Again all was still.

But no, now steps approached. A broken voice said something through the crack in the door. The unfortunate man breathlessly put his ear close and listened. He did not want to see his mother anymore, he just wanted to hear something from her, her last breath, and as he propped himself against the rotten wood, Jochen Wulkow spoke one word from within, dry and rough, "Dead!"

Klas staggered up, the night wind whistled past him, and repeated the ill-fated word. Then everything was still. —

Georg Engel

It was still night when Klas returned home covered in sweat and with turbid hair. The door of his shack stood half open, everything inside was just as he had left it, only the candle stump had burnt down.

He sat down on the chair by the window, squeezed his hands between his knees, and let his head sink down onto his chest.

In his soul, everything had burnt out and been extinguished, only his body twitched from time to time spasmodically.

Outside on the opposite side of the country road stood a solitary poplar, and between its branches and leaves, the moon had hung thin silvery bright nets of light. It flickered and sparkled so strangely that the lonely man's gaze was involuntarily caught in the magical silver threads.

Whether his mother also surely now lingered up there, whether she could surely see him as he sat here with ice-cold feet and crippled heart, he who had sent her up before her time, seduced by unimagined fury, and bewitched by the charming beauty of his wife?

And with the thought of Mieke, it again began to boil in his throat just like before when he had carried out the ill-fated blow.

Had not his mother, his dear, old, dead mother, raised an accusation against her? — But no, the old woman had lied there, he knew it without a doubt. Mieke loved him, and his heart was all tied up at the thought that the consequences of his deed would separate him from her for eternity.

An entire lifetime imprisoned behind walls, behind iron bars, and her perhaps pushed about, misused, dishonoured! —

He raked his hand through his damp sweaty hair and cried out in deathly fear, "Mieke — Mieke, come to me!"

A noise arose.

From the corner in which his mother constantly sat, a figure rose and came slowly nearer. The moonlight trembled over a ghostly white countenance.

"Mieke," the despairing man cried, "have you been sitting there the entire time?"

"Yes, I was waiting for you."

"Mieke, come to me."

She did not stir.

"I want to hold you hand," Klas cried imploringly, "I must leave you, I must leave."

It was as if a cry of dismay had been forced from her lips, but she did not tremble, and offered him her cold fingers. She had become even paler, she kept her eyes half shut.

"If I don't see you again now," Klas began dully, and almost crushed her hand, "Mieke — Mieke — I — have been too fond of you —"

A bitter sobbing choked his words, and his damp forehead sank down onto her hand.

Mieke did not answer. Only after a space of time did she ask with vehement voice, hoarse with horror, "Will they arrest you?"

Klas nodded.

"And me — too?"

"No, Mieke, not you, not you, calm down, you are trembling so, you poor girl," Klas murmured, and drew his wife down to him. Even in his misfortune, he sought only to comfort her.

She now lay before him, destroyed and worn out, only her greenish brown eyes glittered, and glowed up at him in her soul's visible fear.

"And they will determine everything before the court?" she asked with shaking lips, "even the story with the gendarme and me?"

Klas remained silent.

But suddenly he seized his wife by the shoulders, overcame her bristling, and pulled her in an eruption of despair to his chest.

"Is it true?" he howled, looking straight in the face of the heavily breathing creature, "is it true?"

The alarmed woman groaned, crumpled and turned, but he squeezed her as if he wanted to crush her to his chest. Her breath faltered, and in her nameless fear of death, she slung her arms about his neck, and almost bit into his broad, fervent lips.

"It is not true, Klas," she burst out gurgling, "I love you, Klas, I love you."

He breathed deeply, and she fell like a heavy lifeless object from his arms, and remained lying crumpled before him.

"Mieke," he groaned with relief, "I knew it, my sweet Mieke."

For a long time, everything remained still, then finally the young woman rose, and brushed her hair back in deep thought.

"Will you go to the court today?" she inquired after a long hesitation.

He threw a shocked look at her, nodded, and sank into himself again.

Again the same frightened silence, then Mieke peered out onto the brightening village street, and said curtly and decisively, "I will dress and accompany you; wait for me."

Without turning around again, she hurried into her bedroom, and closed the door.

Klas was alone again.

Hour upon hour elapsed, it began to dawn, the heavens extinguished the stars, the moon blurred, the morning wind blew through the branches of the poplars, and awoke a bluethroat which began to chirp quietly, and a weak reddish glow trembled on the panes of the little window. The first red of the sun.

Klas started, his eyes were burning, it was time to fetch Mieke. When he opened the door, he tried to smile; she should not notice how his heart was breaking.

"Mieke!"

No answer.

He rubbed his eyes, and looked around the empty room.

Would she have gone away once more?

Impatiently he stepped to the window and wondered that it was only half ajar. On the window sill lay a piece of rough paper covered with large, awkward letters, and when Klas lifted it up, he recognised immediately that it bore Mieke's handwriting.

Half lacking in will, he lifted it close to his eyes, and read out each word individually:

> To my husband Klas.
> Do not wait for me. I did it, and don't want to go before the judge. Just why did you have to marry me? You are no man, and should have remained with your cantankerous old mother. I don't love the gendarme either, but he is something entirely different. Don't worry abut me. I am running to the city, and won't come back again.
> Mieke.

When Klas had finished reading the letter, he placed the page on the window sill again, and began grinning strangely.

The blow was so monstrous that his weak mind was unable to think the last thing to its end. Not once did a groan force its way over his closed lips, he could only grin, and his cheeks seemed to be paralysed in this terrible grin. Then he fell down onto his bed, burrowed into the pillows, and from time to time, he emitted a ghastly cry, "Mother! Mother!"

How long he lay there, he did not know.

Only when it had become bright as day in the little room did he pull himself together, and look with dull horror into the sun drenched emptiness. — His mother gone, Mieke gone, only he still crouched here, entirely alone, entirely alone. And what did he want to still be here for? Even he must go away, were not the judge and retribution already expecting him?

No more delay.

With wild haste, he tore his cap from the nail, and walked step by step out of the little house. When he closed the door, a thick tear ran over his cheek.

But he had not remained unnoticed. Right before him, at the pump, Jochen Wulkow stood, and seemed occupied with cleaning a small bowl from which he was pouring out water coloured bright red.

"Hey," old Mad Johann called mysteriously, "come here, man."

And Klas staggered over with a shame, with a pained soul, as if this despised village fool were his mightiest, most implacable judge.

"Jochen," he sobbed when he had reached him, and flung his arms around his neck. "I am not as bad as you think, not as bad, not as terribly bad."

"Well, then it's okay," the old man wheezed, freeing himself from his burden arduously, "and now listen, my son, where are you going now?"

Klas did not answer.

"Someone wants to see you first," Mad Johann whispered, and opened his eyes wide. "No, no, let me go on, I want to tell you — your mother came to once more last night."

It seemed to the poor fellow as if a blue flash of lightning had passed down right before his eyes, it twitched and glittered seemingly before his eyes, he lifted his hands high above his head, and broke out into a howl of joy choked by sobs, "What — my mother — lives — Jochen —"

No more words forced themselves from his wheezing chest, but his hand trembled so terribly in that of the old man that the latter felt sympathy with the heavily tried man, and slowly began to inform him, "Yes, last night she came to again," he explained as he let fresh water run into the bowl. "Knew everything exactly, and asked me with such a weak voice for a Bible. — My God, I haven't opened the book in ten years, and when I brought it to her, then she opened it to Paul's epistles, and pointed me to a place which read — wait a moment, my son, yes, which read, 'So ought men to love their wives as their own bodies. He that loveth his wife loveth himself.[2] For this cause shall a man leave his father and mother, and shall be joined unto his wife, and they two shall be one flesh.[3]' And when I read that out to her, Klas, she began to cry and whispered to me that, if she died, then I should tell you she had not stopped loving you. For you were in the right, and she was in the wrong, because she as an old woman had to instruct the young woman over what was good and moral and

---

2   Ephesians 5:28.

3   Ephesians 5:31.

homely. That had been her mistake — and God shall bless you, Klas."

Thus Mad Johann spoke, and wiped his eyes, and felt in his good heart that he had wounded the unfortunate man with a thousand knives.

"And now come with me," he concluded, and led the broken man forcibly away with him.

The sun hovered to their side over the calm sea, the sky was turning blue, and radiating in unending, luminous purity, and a flock of wild, white seagulls fluttered across their path.

They stood before the round, dilapidated clay shack, and when Mad Johann carefully opened the door, it seemed to poor Klas as if his trembling heart would now turn in his chest, his breath faltered, he crept in with lowered head.

The old woman lay on a sordid litter, and had her white head cushioned on a pillow. Her hands were folded on the covers. Nothing moved in this waxen countenance, only the pale lips smiled at the arriving men.

Her son stared at her speechlessly.

"Hanne," Jochen said lovingly, "your son is here."

His mother smiled constantly, always the same good, warm loving smile.

"Hanne, your son, your Klas, just a word — it is all good again."

No movement. But around the hard, old mouth, the forgiving, blissful smile was perpetually encamped.

"My God, Klas — your mother — your mother — does not live anymore," Jochen murmured suddenly, sinking down next to the litter, "dead!"

Again all was still.

The gentle purring of the wind skimming over the shack could be heard.

Then a sound of sorrow that echoed far over the sea, and the giant figure threw himself down before the bed, grasped the stiff hands, kissed them, and screamed out nothing more than the distressingly simple words, "Mother! Mother!"

BLIND

Blind

President: "The defendant is to be led in." And supported diligently by two court servants, a short, white-haired gentleman strides into the jury court of the north German coastal town, fingers the defendants bench carefully, and then slowly sits down.

He is clothed neatly, painfully neatly, his delicate hands are covered by black lambskin gloves, and his snow white hair is parted strictly in the middle.

The smooth shaven, distinguished countenance whose soft features betray his good education is borne high and upright by him.

A murmur goes through the room, then it is deathly still again.

"The man is blind," the President says, and instinctively closes his eyes, and as his words fade away, a young, blond, entirely black dressed woman down on the witness bench shudders fearfully, and her timid, imploring look is riveted for minutes on the motionless old man up there.

Her heart, the wild, fierce thing in her chest, beats faster and faster, more and more eyes seem to be directed at her, and the dead pupils of the blind man speak to her more and more mysteriously.

Like black figures of the Inquisition, the judges sit around her, a sombre, breathless silence all around, and on the green table, dully lit by the two candles, a silver effigy of the saviour gleams.

Did not a round, glowing red drop of blood really drip over its transfixed feet?

She wants to scream, then a calm, clear voice hinders her.

President: "You are the Senator Karl Christoph Valenus?"

Defendant: "Yes, President."

President: "How old?"

Defendant: "53 years."

President: "You are blind?"

Defendant: "Yes."

President: "Can you recall when you met this misfortune?"

Defendant: "Ten years ago."

President: "You have been married just as long too?"

Defendant: "Just as long."

President: "Your wife was the daughter of your best friend. I read from your files that you were nursed by the lady during your long illness, that you then married her and have lived in happy, unclouded marriage."

The beautiful, pale woman on the witness bench leans back exhausted, and closes her eyes.

Something like paralysis runs through her body, and she only hears the calm voice of her husband as if it is coming through a thick haze, "Yes, President, it is all as you say."

President: "Defendant, you, up to now one of the most highly esteemed men of the town, stand here before the jury to answer for a murder. One evening you surrendered yourself to the Coroner, and announced that you had shot your young friend, Baron von Bibritz, from behind. At the time, you refused any explanation of this mysterious case. Do you also still stand by your silence today?"

Defendant (firmly): "I have admitted to the deed, President. Everything else leave with me."

President: "Defendant, do you also have straight in your mind what the consequences of your decision are?

If you do not lift the veil for us, if we do not learn anything of the motives which drove you to your ill-fated deed, then, Mr Valenus, the verdict of the court must fall fatally for you. But let me caution you once more! We are all convinced that deep inner reasons have been astir, that it perhaps was even a misunderstood matter of honour which ruled over you. Senator, you are blind, no colour shines for you, eternal night surrounds you, such a man does not seize the weapon out of malign murderous intent. Speak, explain yourself —"

Defendant (uncertain): "You will not learn anything more, President. I beg you once more, come to a decision."

And the President broke off the questioning.

Then the Crown Prosecutor spoke, shortly after the Defence Counsel, the jury withdrew, and then slowly strode back into the room.

The head of the jury read out the verdict, "Guilty — mitigating circumstances are allowed."

"And guilty, guilty," it shrieked as if with a thousand voices in the ears of the blond lady there below.

With wide-open eyes, she stared at the silver crucifix.

No, it is no longer the reflection of the flickering light, the saviour moves, and shakes his fist at her, and from the cross it booms, "Guilty, guilty."

She collapses in a faint.

President: "The Defendant is sentenced to five years in prison."

***

Four years elapsed, then the District Court President received one day a sealed letter from the prison in N—.

It contained the short statement of the institute's Director that a few days before, No. 54, the former Senator Valenus, had died.

Immediately before his parting, he had presented to an officer the enclosed letter for the President.

Surprised and shocked, the recipient read the following.

Blind

It all happened in this way! It was a long, long time ago, a good fifteen years. (Oh! Since I cannot see anymore, every day stretches to eternity.)

I awoke and rubbed my eyes, but strangely, everything remained night, and yet I knew it must be day.

I grasped at my bed, it was there — I groped for my watch, it lay in its usual place and was ticking quickly and loudly.

Strange — I hastily threw myself back into the pillows, and pressed my head against the wall.

I still thought that it was all an ugly, black dream, only, while I held my eyes shut, my heart pounded so wildly, so fearfully that I leapt up after a short time.

Night again, calm, impenetrable night from which nothing emerged.

I laughed out loud, and clutched my head. I distinctly heard this laugh, but I did not comprehend that it was me, and was startled by it.

For a moment I remained quite still.

It must return, the wistfully expected light, I felt its warmth, sensed even that sparkling, hot sunbeams were playing on my cheek.

Now something was humming about my head, it came closer and closer until I recognised the noise of a buzzing fly.

It sat down on my hand, but I did not see it. I was still sitting motionlessly; I did not believe it, and pondered over it.

Before I had lain down to rest the day before, guests had lingered at my place.

I did not know exactly, I had seen though, fastened with both eyes, my old friend and Lilli, his daughter!

Lilli had worn a blue dress.

So, blue.

I must have seen that it was blue.

Oh, how this knowledge calmed me!

If I had still distinguished the colours yesterday, then my current incapability must have quite natural causes. Certainly, I had merely awoken earlier, and it was still night!

Then a terrible thought shuddered through me.

I want to light a candle. —

Yes, that is it — light — then I will see.

Trembling, I felt for the candlestick, but so strong was my agitation that I knocked it down, and only the matchsticks remained in my hand.

I struck one, it broke.

The second flared up.

How did I know that?

Woe — I did not see it, I felt only the small flame, felt it until it singed my finger.

I unconsciously struck another, and another, burnt the entire box, and the smell of the singed wood smelt doubly strong in my nose.

A monstrous fury seized me.

I sprung from my bed, threw myself down in the middle of the floor, and leapt up again.

There in the corner, a full bowl stood on the wash stand.

I put myself to rights, and dipped my entire head in the cool water, I tore my eyes open and let the fluid penetrate into them.

Then I looked around anew.

Night, night, night —

Blind

I screamed, roared for hours, finally I started again, I felt a soft hand rest on my forehead, and heard from a voice for the first time the decisive words, "He is blind."

***

She sat next to me.

I had raged and blustered for two months, now I awoke to a new consciousness.

Lilli sat next to me as the wild fever fled from me.

She bent over me, I felt her breath playing about my forehead coolingly, and suddenly I embraced her, and pressed her sobbing to my chest.

Oh, how I praise you still today, compassionate tears which she shed at the time.

They flowed into my eyes like beneficial, miraculous pearls, they calmed me, and I no longer cursed the night which surrounded me. And yet — I was a blustering, lunatic fool!

Shortly before my misfortune, I had engaged myself to Lilli, now I was egotistical enough to presume her sacrifice.

It was in the large, beautiful, deep garden behind my house.

For the first time I sat again in the woven bamboo chair, and listened to the nightingale sing.

They blared about joy and love, and the flowers gave off their scent, and the treetops murmured, and the sunbeams scurried over golden green lawn — but I was blind.

And again Lilli sat next to me, and her hand rested in mine.

Then the realisation came over me once more, "Leave me, Lilli, you are so young and beautiful, and I have become a blind old man. I don't want your sacrifice."

She squeezed my hand, and remained silent.

"You cannot love me, Lilli."

She threw herself on my chest, and sobbed loudly, "I feel sympathy with you, boundless sympathy which tears my heart up — I cannot leave you."

Then I exulted, fool me, who wanted to shackle the living to the numb.

Fool me, fool me — I was blind!

Blind

The years crept along, and as night after night came every new day for me.

We lived in solitude in the large house, only occasionally were we visited by the young Baron Bibritz, an estate owner with whom I was connected in business.

I had liked him, for he was the most honest man I had ever met in my life.

But most of the time he delighted me by his splendid, sonorous organ, and so it happened that he often had to read aloud to me for hours. For some time, he came daily, then more seldom, finally he stayed away completely.

Only after I did not encounter him anymore at my place did I feel a strong yearning for him, and it forced me to at least speak about him a lot.

"Lilli, doesn't this strange disappearance make you fret too?" I asked my wife one day, who, seemingly occupied with work of some sort, was sitting by the window.

She did not answer straight away, but then she said calmly, "No, Christoph, he will be busy."

Only I was not yet satisfied, but had to converse even longer about my friend.

"He is a handsome man, Lilli," I asked, "don't you think so?"

She always answered with the same calmness and kindliness.

Oh, her gentle voice, how mellow it sounded to me.

"Yes, he is very handsome, Christoph."

"And his hair, blond or brown?"

"Brown."

"How comes it that we have never spoken about it; do you like him then?"

I heard her pack up her knitting, and straight afterwards she responded quickly, "My judgment is not authoritative; but I also consider him to be a respectable character, and take pleasure in particular when he honours you with his presence. Perhaps he will come again soon."

She almost seemed to have foreseen it.

That afternoon when I awoke from sleep, I thought I discerned the Baron's voice.

I called him joyfully, only my cry enticed Lilli over, who assured me that I must have been deceived.

In the evening, he really came.

My wife had complained of a headache beforehand, and had withdrawn in good time.

So we were alone.

He sat down opposite me, and sought to excuse his long absence, and I had to secretly laugh that he did it so awkwardly.

"Business? — — Empty excuses," I suddenly mocked, "You certainly utilised your time better — perhaps it is even a love?"

The Baron remained silent for a moment, and I heard how he rocked back and forth on his chair, then he replied uncertainly, "Yes, it is a love, Senator!"

"So then —"

I laughed ungovernably over my good idea, and mocked him with all my strength.

Finally I asked why he had not drawn me, his friend, into his trust earlier.

"Because it is a dangerous affection," he responded, and his deep voice shook — "it concerns a married woman."

I started. "But are you mad then, Baron? And you announce that so openly? — — Hopefully the woman concerned knows nothing yet of your love?"

"Yes, she knows!"

"And she loves you back?"

"Yes, yes!"

"And — ?"

"Nothing more," he broke off, and rose. "We will return to our reading again."

He then read to me for almost the entire evening, although I could not collect my thoughts at all.

He left me later than usual. Alone, I did not get any rest in my bed; again and again, the thought of my friend's strange revelation chased me, and I sat at the coffee table the next morning still incessantly occupied by it.

An evil longing took hold of me to share it, for since I had received eternal darkness in my eyes, I had to speak, I had to hear voices, I could not close myself off anymore.

Lilli was lingering again in her usual place when I ferried the ill-fated words, "Now I know why the Baron has been neglecting us for so long. He loves a married woman! Would you have believed it, Lilli?" — —

Something fell clattering to the floor, I was startled, and I felt seemingly as if she were looking at my empty pupils.

Then she stammered something, and scurried past me.

And through her flight through the wide room, I heard distinctly a female voice sobbing deeply and passionately. —

But no, I must have been deceived, for only a few minutes later, she returned, placed some refreshments down before me, and was able to joke over my news.

We chatted for a long time, only when the servant appeared with the newspapers did she rise, and step down into the garden.

I remained alone with my old steward.

I was in a strange mood, something cold trickled down my back, and in my eyes, something burned, horribly agonising, like molten lead.

I could not escape the thought, it tormented me, — she had sobbed.

The tone transfixed my ear like a sharp knife. And then came the decision.

I called my servant, pretended that the Baron had written to me over some lost object, and asked him to recall when my friend had last been there.

"But Senator," the old man said smiling, "the Baron comes almost daily."

"Dai— ?" — I began suddenly laughing so loud that the servant was worried about me, but I calmed him down, and sent him away.

Then I rose anew to laughing, exactly like the time when I had awoken and the night had not wanted to go away, the night — the night — — —

Oh, but I was very well; I sat there, and giggled, and bit myself on the hands, and stood up, and walked about in the darkness.

In the afternoon, I found after a long groping about in my drawers the revolver which had lain in its place for years.

Towards evening my wife complained suddenly over renewed pains, and withdrew again.

Half an hour later, my friend arrived.

The servant placed a lamp on the table for us, and the Baron continued his reading aloud without further preliminaries.

I lay half numb in my armchair, and did not listen to anything he read.

But in my eyes, the drops became hotter and hotter and more and more seething, I wanted to groan, but I was frightened of startling the Baron, and remained silent.

Towards ten o'clock, he rose and wanted to curtly take his leave.

I held him back; now it had to happen!

"Why are you robbing me of your society so early," I asked, forcibly containing myself, "or did you perhaps have to go to that lady?"

I heard his quick breath, then he said fiercely, "Guess!"

"Are you expected?"

I clasped onto the table firmly, and noticed how the lamp trembled on the wood.

"Yes," he said uncertainly. "For the first time —"

For a span of time, it remained still between us, then he stretched out his hand to me, and wished me a calm 'good night!'

Now he would go!

Slowly I rose, and intentionally pushed the book to the floor.

"Pick it up," I commanded curtly.

He willingly bent down to it, and at the same time in thanks, I tapped him gently on the shoulder.

"What a broad back he has," I thought, then I squeezed off — — —

***

My days are coming to an end.

I will die in prison.

Only now do I know that all men are blind, only death makes them see!

A DEAL

The Deal

Dark mist was drawing across the sea. It veiled the pale sinking disc of the sun in a sombre web, it crept up the white chalk cliffs like black sea ghosts wanting to fight against the light, and then plunged soundlessly down into the dark valleys of the lonely island's dunes.

And it became dark and night; through the serious fir forests which drew black and menacing around the deserted bay, a gust of wind blew; a rustle passed through the treetops, and down below, the water swished an answer, short and cutting.

The sea so still, the forest so sombre, and the mist climbing and climbing until everything, everything is a single, dark haze.

It only sparkled and twitched on the outermost tips of the dunes, like a light which flickers fearfully in the wind.

A man was striding along the beach and looked up into the flickering shimmer of light.

He paid no attention to the endless black sea which crept nearer and ever nearer and washed his feet, he stared anxiously at the reddish glow up there, and when the little flame twitched, then his step faltered, his feet became leaden as if they did not want to carry him anymore up into the poor fisherman's cottage, up into that little room which he had to reach if he wanted to find some rest.

There! — did something not roar and echo from across the sea?

A wave struck surging on the sand, and he started.

It seemed to him as if out there a ghostly voice had called her name. — Her name — Herta! —

He shook himself and grasped his chest.

Yes, there in the thick, leather pouch lay the money, the heavy, fearfully gathered money; it lay there, and pressed against his heart.

And again the little light flickered, and he strode on with lowered head.

The man was the young ship's pilot Swen Bögen.

*****

Up in the wooden quarters, the old fisherman Wilm Gäde sat on the bench by the stove and mended nets.

He had lowered his massive, fat head with the grey turned moustache and large, crooked mouth onto his chest, and he only occasionally squinted under his bushy eyebrows over at his daughter Herta who was sitting at the table and had propped her head on her arms. A sandy-haired plait fell over her shoulders, and in the glow of the burning candle stump, her eyes sparkled.

She was beautiful.

It remained quiet between them for a long time; the old man threw the nets back and forth, and the girl scratched the table with her nails.

They would not have spoken to each other for a long time if a seagull had not flown past their window cawing.

The daughter started. The old man also squinted at her.

"Boring, mending," he said, "tell me something."

"I don't know anything, father."

The old man jerked at the nets and fell silent for a moment, then he demanded anew, "Tell me the story of Swen Bögen."

His voice surely sounded rough and commanding, but the girl bent defiantly over the table and balled her fists.

"No," she responded brusquely, — "I must tell you every day — it hurts me!"

"I want it to," Wilm growled in response and shoved his hulking head forward slowly towards the light. — "Since the great flood when your mother drowned and your sisters, I have had a heavy head and forget everything — don't hear it — I want to know about Swen Bögen again — !" Thus he began, "Swen Bögen came over on the ship as a helmsman and lived with Wilm Gäde. — How long was he there?"

"Eight weeks and a day," Herta whispered, and again scratched vehemently at the table.

"Yes," the old man repeated. — "And one day — and then he seduced you —"

The girl turned blood-red.

"I was good to him, father."

"Bad," the blockhead growled, and thrust his heavy waterproof boots against the table so that it creaked. "Eight weeks and a day he was here, and one day I knocked on his room's door, but he did not open. You were inside."

She cried out, "He had promised me he wanted to take me as his wife."

"Yes, he promised you that. — And what do the people say?"

The girl pressed her hands to her breast and sank back breathlessly into her wooden chair. — After a while, however, she spoke sombrely, "He went away. The people say that he married the ship's pilot's widow and God pre— —"

But she did not finish, instead she sprang up, and said curtly, "Now that's enough — now I have told you it again!"

"Swen Bögen!" the old man murmured furiously.

And again it became quite still, only the little light twitched and flickered, and from the coastal forest, a creaking and groaning arose.

Herta had strode into the corner to shake out the old man's litter, and meanwhile Wilm Gäde stretched out his arms and yawned.

It was an ugly picture when the old man tore open his crooked, almost toothless mouth.

"When he returns," he erupted in a strange tone, "I will drown him."

"Who?" Herta started from her brooding.

"Swen Bögen. He broke his word."

"Yes, so."

She asked nothing further, for otherwise her father would tell the eternal story of the promise which he had given his wife's brother when that man had lain on his deathbed, and that he considered his undoing.

But he had promised his brother-in-law that he would care for his wife and child, and when the great flood came, then he had thought of it and had, his youngest on his arm, hurried to the forsaken. Then when he had returned home to find his cottage had collapsed, wife and children drowned, a post had broken off the rotten beams and had fallen on his head.

"He isn't coming," Herta murmured as she patted out the last seaweed pillow, and as she said it, the sand crunched outside, and a stone rolled against the door.

There was a knock on the door.

"Open it," the old man said, "it is the smith."

Reluctant about the late visitor, she approached the door and pulled the bolt back.

A slender man with short cropped blond hair stepped into the circle of light and stretched out his hand to her.

Then she went as white as snow.

"It is Swen Bögen," she said breathlessly.

No further greeting welcomed him, no hand pushed a chair towards the exhausted man, the three people stood wordlessly and stared, only Herta's quick breath filled the cottage.

And Swen Bögen's eyes sought her own.

He thought of how beautiful she had been that time in his room, and how the sea had raced at her feet and roared.

Then he hastily grasped his chest to check if the money was still pressing against his heart — and right — it was there.

A dull growl interrupted the silence, then Wilm Gäde rose ponderously and lifted his hulking head up three or four times so that the veins on his neck swelled.

"What do you want, Swen?" he asked over-sweetly.

When he heard the familiar voice, the fear fell away from the ship's pilot, and he could scratch irritably behind his ear and answer, "I want to finally have some rest, no more roaming about for me, no more talk of the water for me — I want reconciliation!"

The old man smirked, but the girl to whom it was all said just threw him a single glance, then she turned to the window and clenched her teeth. Instead of her, the old man hauled himself over to the new arrival and placed his balled fist on his shoulder.

"Reconciliation?" he repeated in a low voice. "What are you offering me for it, Swen?"

The blond man faltered.

Again Wilm Gäde lifted his fist, and his crooked mouth began to twitch.

"What are you offering?" he whispered menacingly.

Then the other man let out a deep sigh and burst out hoarsely, "I offer you two hundred taler. More I don't have. I scraped it together until it was all there. I also stayed over there for the money. I do it in spite of myself. My mother brought me into the world when a hundred taler lay on the table. She looked at it all night. It is in my blood."

"Count it out," Wilm Gäde said.

Hesitantly the ship's pilot pulled out the pouch, hesitantly he counted banknotes and gold pieces out onto the table, and the gold sparkled and glistened when the beams of light glided over it.

"One is still missing," the old man laughed greedily.

The stranger searched, but he could not find the last one anymore. He shrugged his shoulders irritably.

"It is the same," he murmured, "take it, it is enough."

"But it is not two hundred," Wilm Gäde smiled teasingly.

While the young ship's pilot stood there as if he could not part from the metallic gleam, the old man gathered the entire heap with his large hand and shoved it all in his pocket.

"A deal is a deal," he slurred.

"And you, Herta, say it too," Swen demanded and stepped up behind the girl who was looking soundlessly through the window into the night.

A gust of wind blew in the chimney, and a howling ran over the cottage.

Then the lonely girl turned, and looked at her seducer for the first time. His avaricious eyes sparkled like two dull pieces of gold.

"It is your last business," she suddenly cried rejoicingly, but as he stepped back in shock, she grasped the candle stump, nodding her head, and remained standing waiting in the doorway.

"Lead him into the room," the old man ordered, sitting sunken in himself on the bench by the stove, and jingling the money. "Swen is our guest. When must you leave?"

The ship's pilot became uncomfortable. "A day ago," he said curtly, and quickly climbed up the small staircase which led up to that room.

The girl, however, remained standing in the open door and held the candle high above her head to light his way; the glow fell brightly on her white arm from which the broad sleeve had fallen back, and it seemed also as if individual sparks of light were gliding over her sandy hair.

Then his step died away, and Herta turned curtly to her father. Her countenance was ghostly pale.

"Will he die?" she whispered hoarsely.

The old man was still jingling the money, only after a long pause did he mutter mysteriously, "Swen Bögen broke his word — Swen Bögen has broken it again, for his money is not all there. He shall drown like your mother and your sisters drowned — tomorrow morning — and now quiet."

Humming, he undressed, threw himself on the litter, and after a few minutes, he was snoring.

But outside black clouds were flying across the sky, and only a single star floated between them, and its image trembled in the sea like a bluish silver taler.

***

What was that creaking there? What was crossing through the room?

Everything was dark and still, but now it stirred again.

Swen Bögen had thrown himself clothed onto the bed, now he straightened up and called fearfully, "Who is there?"

No answer, but then — did it not scrape again?

A cry of fear left him. Yes, there something cracked, a bluish light flickered as if someone was using a matchstick, and now he saw with his startled eyes that Herta stood before him, a candle in her brown hand.

He stared in bewilderment at her, and straightened up fully without knowing what he was doing.

It felt so strangely dreamlike to him that he could not think whether a long time had elapsed between then and now. —

Again she held the candle in her trembling hand, again wondrous shadows scurried over the rotten furniture, and through the window, a blue star was flickering from an infinite distance!

A noise interrupted his thoughts. She was holding the candle quite closely before her eyes as if she wanted to shine it down to the ground.

"Do you love her?" she asked calmly.

"Who?"

"The one over there — your wife?"

Swen Bögen rocked back and forth on the edge of the bed, and gnawed his lip. Then he said hastily, "She is rich, hence I am good to her. But not like with you; I don't know how it happens. You only love once!"

As he said it, he looked at her, at her bare feet, and at her gleaming hair, then he struck both hands together, and whistled through his teeth, "Herta!"

"What do you want, Swen Bögen?"

"You don't like me anymore, do you?"

"Yes, yes, I love you, Swen!"

He cried out aloud, and drew her to himself.

She flung her arms around his neck. Oh! How cold her mouth was, how her limbs shook against his own.

"Why are you frightened?" he asked.

Then she laughed, and yet her teeth were audibly chattering against each other.

"I am not frightened," she laughed wildly. "This time you will be true to me, for you will die in your love!"

Once more Swen Bögen was startled, once more a horror penetrated through him, then her lips met his, and something like fire and fervour broke in through the horror and fear.

The expiring candle was the last thing he saw.

***

"Here is the taler, I found it still in the pouch."

With these words, the ship's pilot approached before sunrise the litter on which Wilm Gäde was still squatting drowsily.

The old man coolly grasped the gold piece and pocketed it. —

"That is something else," he yawned. — "Now the deal is closed, my son."

"I must go," Swen Bögen urged uneasily, and the girl, waiting stiff and upright by the door, added coldly, almost cruelly, "It is time — take him away, father!"

They started off.

When they stepped out onto the dunes, Herta strode ahead, the old man remained somewhat back with the ship's pilot.

And they came closer and closer to the enormous chalk cliffs which plunged down in abrupt descents, steep and jagged to the sea. Below, the white foam roared against the rock, digging and burrowing, it flooded back again and then raced up anew. Entire flocks of white seagulls whirled over the white spray, a sharp crag raised its dripping head from the whirlpool, and floating wreaths of kelp and seaweed swirled about down there in narrow circles.

Here it must happen!

Herta shuddered and stopped as though spellbound. She already felt the last push, she heard the howling in the air which the falling body would cut through — and there below, the crag, the pointed, horrible one, was it not already coloured red and bloody?

She wanted to scream, but the air had left her; stiff, incapable of words, she had to watch the two men approaching.

And now — now they were next to her.

The two figures towered clearly and sharply into the blue sky — a moment still, and the old man stepped behind Swen.

Herta turned earthly pale, and closed her eyes. But it still twitched back and forth under her closed eyelashes like red blood.

"Farewell!" Swen Bögen's voice suddenly intoned.

She staggered up.

Was it really so? And was that old Wilm, her father, who lingered idly in the distance?

"Farewell!" the ship's pilot said once more.

It was no cry anymore, it was a shriek which was forced from the girl's throat.

"Father, father!"

A cry of ruination and destruction. The cliff threw it back, and the wild lament shrilled across the sea.

The old man heard it, and shook his massive head indifferently, then he called across, "He has paid, and the deal is settled; Swen Bögen goes!"

"Farewell," the ship's pilot urged for a third time and grasped the hand of his beloved.

He had still not seized her fingers when she pushed him back and sprang to the edge of the cliff.

A quick look up at the room where she had been so happy — she raised her arms up high over her head and plunged, head forward, into the depths.

A swishing, a blow, a scream, and the green kelp wreath down there was dancing and circling around a pale, bloody countenance.

"Help!" Swen Bögen cried, beside himself.

The Deal

From below, a cutting wind came up, the old insane Wilm leant out over the abyss.

Not for long, then he stepped back and murmured, "You have paid me, Swen Bögen, and the deal is settled, but see down there: she was my last."

A PLEDGE

The narrow, green stream crept idly to the sea. Glistening water lilies floated past, small sticks drove past, and sometimes blue, brown, and rosy spots appeared on the water, issuing from dripping tar.

It was early in the morning.

On the small cargo boat fastened to the worm-eaten brown bulwark with iron chains, bustling dominated.

The three sons of the mariner Christoph Holmsen stood on the deck, and let down into the hold the massive, misshapen wool bales which the small boat would bring to the Danish coast tomorrow, to Korsör.

The work was hard, and the three blond heroic figures worked restlessly.

No words were exchanged, no joke made, the large loads plunged incessantly into the depths. But though they did not converse, the three nevertheless thought for each other.

The two youngest kept count of the number of bales, according to which their wages were judged, and Jürgen, the eldest, heard here the waves of the sea swishing on the quiet water, he already saw the small boat flying along, far over the deserted surface, like the white heron, and over on the emerging beach —

He sighed as he loaded the heaviest of the bales onto his back.

He should not think of it, and yet, he saw her too distinctly. How she stood over there, the red-headed Göde with the white full arms, as if she awaited him so as to embrace him again like that time when she had not yet betrayed him.

A shudder shook Jürgen's body so strongly that he had to sit down on one of the bales.

Then his father stood before him, a powerful man with a twisted grey beard. A mariner's cap covered his large head.

"What's wrong, Jürgen?"

His son looked up, taken aback, and turned blood-red, "Father — I — let me steer the boat," he asked imploringly.

"No — you are staying at home this time," the old man said definitely.

"Father, I beg you!"

"You are staying!"

The blond hero clasped the mariner's arm and began whispering, "I will not meet Göde again, I promise you — only I must be at sea, it is to narrow for me here."

"And you will go to your hussy again," the old man countered sedately, and rocked his head; "as soon as you touch the yellow sand over there, you will do it. You will see her, and then you will forget that when she was your fiance, she went down, not with one, no, with many, many, and the disgrace will be there. No, it is fortunate that the hussy has moved over there with her parents, you should leave her there. And now to work!"

"So you are refusing me?"

"You heard."

"Good!"

The work resumed restlessly, and the old man strode onto land again to his small cottage.

But his dictum had not soothed his eldest, instead Jürgen called together his brothers at midday, and as he wiped off the sweat with the coarse sackcloth, he burst out stuttering, "You heard everything before. Now you will speak with father. I must go out or I will become ill."

In the afternoon, Jürgen's mother came to the boat.

She was a small, round woman who constantly stroked her hands and shook her head to every word.

"Jürgen," she said softly, "father is angry with you."

"Beg for me," he cried to her desperately, "beg for me, mother!"

The tall, blond fellow was her favourite, hence she twisted her hands anxiously, murmured several times, "bad, bad," and pattered onto land again.

It became evening.

The river turned dark and black, and from the distant mouth, a stronger roar sounded. The three brothers locked the hold and now strode to their father's house.

In the rectangular, cabin-like space, the mariner's family then sat down to supper.

Everyone enjoyed their portion in silence, they did not appear to be accustomed to conversation, then the four men lit their pipes, and soon thick, blue haze hovered about the ancient lamp.

A strong smell of tobacco filled the cottage, everything blurred into dancing clouds, and only the knitting needles of Jürgen's mother could still be heard distinctly clattering away. They sat thus until the clock hidden in the haze struck the tenth hour.

Now the mother rose first, then the two younger brothers stood up, and they all took themselves to bed with a short farewell. Old Christoph Holmsen and his eldest remained alone.

For a moment, the two remained silent, then the old man took his pipe from his mouth.

"Jürgen," he rasped, "come here."

The son obeyed.

The old man also rose, and opened the small, low window out which the blue haze escaped. Then old

Holmsen placed his hand on his son's shoulder, and said almost sorrowfully, "Jürgen, you shall go out."

"Father!" the youth cried out jubilantly.

But the mariner continued, "You shall go out because you spoke of sickness. That shall not be! But on one thing, I want an oath and handshake. You shall not speak to nor touch this hussy, this Göde. That is it."

Jürgen fetched a deep breath, his eyes sparkled, his heart trembled, and he spoke nonetheless, "I swear, father, I swear to you."

"Not here," the mariner sighed, — "I want the oath there before the picture."

A large engraving, brown with age, looked down from the opposite wall.

It portrayed the saviour as he walked across the waters, and the sinking Peter who implored him to save him. The sun sparkled above the head of the saviour, otherwise everything was veiled in darkness, and the waves struck greedily at the fear-filled young man.

When old Holmsen looked up there, his weathered face brightened, and he nodded in greeting as though honouring an old acquaintance.

He had his own background with the picture.

Many years before, when his sons had still been children, the mariner had suffered a shipwreck between the island and the mainland. The waves had plunged roaring on his head, the north wind had flung him roaring into the depths, and the sea had whirled him about as though in a monstrous, gurgling maelstrom. His breath had already left him, a thousand red sparks danced about his eyes, then — a starry bright apparition appeared before his dazzled senses.

It had seemed to him as if the Lord Jesus Christ was surging towards him, exactly like he floated over the sea in the picture. And the saviour had offered him his hand and spoken, "I am helping you." —

When old Holmsen had at the time come to again, he was lying on the deck of a coal ship which had fished up the drifting man. The convalescent did not forget his divine rescuer, however.

Hardly had he returned to his small hometown that he bought the picture of the saviour striding over the sea without wetting the hem of his clothes, and the engraving was treated by the entire family from then on as a relic.

You shall swear it here," the old man said solemnly and raised his hand up stiffly, "you shall make an oath that you will neither speak to nor touch the hussy."

"Neither speak to nor touch," Jürgen repeated, turning pale as chalk, "I swear."

The old man looked into his son's face for a moment, then his lips began to tremble, and he murmured worriedly, "If you are lying, then the saviour will pass in a storm over the sea and will seize you."

"I am not lying," Jürgen said firmly.

The old man nodded.

"I know," he affirmed, "and now, good night and farewell! You will already be at sea at five o'clock."

He drew his eldest to his heart, and what he had never done before, he pressed his bearded mouth onto the shaking lips of the younger man.

"Farewell —"

***

Like a lonely seagull floating close above the water seeking food, the little ship swept across the still sea.

The prow rose sometimes as if it wanted to greet the rising green land with jubilant breast, and thousands of whirling flowers of foam pearled up about the keel.

The land climbed higher and higher, and now thousands of white spraying waves surged up as if they were bringing the young skipper the first greetings — oh, the first greetings from her.

"Neither speak to nor touch," he murmured to himself.

He had thought of the ill-fated words during the entire trip, he was still thinking of them when they came into the broad, silted up harbour.

But soon the work captivated him.

He had to diligently bring the load into the store with the owner's people, and his brothers bustled about him cheerfully.

The third hour was already approaching amidst jokes and song.

"Jürgen," a laughing voice suddenly said behind him.

All the blood surged into his face, the heavy bales swayed in his arms, he had almost collapsed.

But he took hold of himself, and turned to where the voice came from.

He wanted to be strong, only look at the most beautiful, the most faithless woman on earth once, and then turn away for eternity.

There on the broad plank which bound the bulwark and the ship together stood a voluptuous girl's figure, Göde. —

Sandy plaits framed her head, her arms and cheeks blossomed rosy and white, and from her eyes flashed ardent, bluish fire.

She was bewilderingly beautiful, and she smiled because she saw at first sight that Jürgen was again immersed in the sweet, unfathomable sea which surged in her eyes.

He stood speechlessly.

"Jürgen!" the brothers called impatiently.

Then she spoke to him.

"I saw from our window how you came in, and recognised you straightaway. Give me your hand, Jürgen."

At the same time, she stepped forward far across the plank, and stretched her fingers towards him so that she almost touched his.

"Give."

He bent down a little, all his limbs were shaking, everything was compelling him to those cherry red lips. Everything was forgotten.

"Neither speak to nor touch!"

Jürgen started, then he squeezed his eyes shut, and turned back to his work.

Göde laughed. "Don't you want to answer me?" she inquired, shrugging her shoulders.

But he was not paying attention to her anymore, and with clenched teeth, he continued working.

Every attempt to make conversation with the blond hero failed. Astonished, confused, Göde beat a retreat. But she came again. Sometimes she was sashaying close by the side of the boat, other times she rowed past below in a dinghy, another time she stood in the distance, and looked yearningly at the boat.

And Jürgen followed her under his lowered eyelashes, but he acted as if he did not notice her.

Then the girl suddenly vanished.

Hours had passed, behind them the sun had sunken into the sea, a cool wind was skimming over it, and up above on the dark, steely disc of the heavens, the golden stars were appearing. The moon spread a silvery carpet over the deck.

Jürgen's brothers had long ago climbed onto land to look for a sailors' bar where fun was to be had. They had begged for his accompaniment imploringly, but the young skipper did not want to incur the temptation, and now guarded the slumbering boat alone.

He huddled back on the roof of the cabin, and stared up into the dark, endless dome in which the small golden fires burned.

If the sparkling constellation of the bear up there were to fade, then he would have to wind up the anchor, and the boat would fly homewards, empty and unladen, just like his own heart which was likewise abandoning here its last treasure.

Oh, how beautiful the girl was, how luminous her arms, how her lips had once rested on his own. And now — betrayed, all over — neither speak to nor touch.

Something rustled on the boat, a shadow glided over the moonlit deck, a rope end fell to the deck.

Jürgen looked up, and in the same moment, a soft arm placed itself around his neck, and a voice urged ardently and fretfully, "Jürgen, won't you forgive me?"

As if a mermaid had touched him, he sat for a moment stiff and motionless, but then he pushed back roughly, and turned his feverish countenance to the heavens again.

The red-headed Göde remained standing before him, and wrung her hands imploringly, "Then at least speak to me!" she burst out passionately. "You know I love you still despite everything!"

He sat silently opposite her.

Then she suddenly crouched at his feet, sobbing loudly, forced herself on him so that he felt the warmth of this beautiful body, and as she clasped his arms, she murmured timidly, "Jürgen, I cannot help that I have become what I am now. It has lain in me as long as I can remember. But I can only love you. I want nothing more from you, nothing, nothing at all, I just want to be permitted to cuddle and kiss you once more. Just once more."

She rose fiercely on her knees, her ardent mouth thirsting for him, and she drew him down with almost superhuman force.

He screamed out loud, the blood hummed and seethed in his veins, but then he tore himself away from her, and threw himself wailing on the flat roof of the cabin. No word had passed over his lips, he had kept his pledge.

Without farewell, with a dull sigh, Göde turned away, and hurried like a fluttering bird to the gangplank.

He saw already how she stepped onto the plank, already her luminous hair was blurring into the darkness, then he could no longer hold himself.

A spring, he seized her shoulders.

"Göde!"

"Dear?" she exulted.

"Do you love me?"

In the moonlight, her rosy cheeks glowed, her lips opened, her youthful breast shook stormily against him. Then she embraced him as if she wanted to strangle him.

"Only you," she stammered, half senseless.

Their lips pressed against each others, he lifted the girl up, and let her down slowly.

About the boat, however, the waves were swishing.

***

The sea cracked thunderingly against the planks of the returning boat.

The north wind struck with grisly howls into the raging water so that monstrous white steeds sprang up from its chasms, chasing the groaning boat about with fluttering manes.

It was day, and yet the sky threatened black and dark, the chalk cliffs stretched their white bodies like enormous giants out of the black haze, and the surf which raced against its feet was the voice of this unlovely being, and boomed eerily over the surface.

The elements were in revolt, it seethed, raged, sprayed, and devoured itself in grim fury.

"Take the sail down!" Jürgen's brothers called fearfully.

"Wheel around!" cried another. "Perhaps we can return."

But their words were drowned out by the storm, and still Jürgen stood at the helm with head uncovered, and held course for home.

And as loud as the sea roared, as much as the storm curved the sail so that every yard sang a discordant dirge, his heart flew still more fearfully and stormily in his chest.

Yes, he understood what the white giants there were roaring with brazen voices over the waters, "You shall not speak to the girl nor touch her. Woe, the saviour is already travelling over the waters and will seize you."

A groaning went through the ship's skeleton, the storm broke a sail with doubled fury, and threw the spars crashing down.

"Careful! — Jürgen, you were hit."

It was only a blow which he received from a falling yard onto the head. He did not stagger once from it, his senses only clouded over for a moment, and like a jerking flash of lightning, all his thoughts flew back to the cosy cabin in which he had held the beautiful woman in his arms the night before!

Impenetrable night had accumulated around the little boat in the meantime, an endless black waste full of horror stretched out before the mariners.

It soon flew up into the sky, then it submerged again into the maelstrom, fizzing water plunged over the boat and threw it on its side.

A cry for help sounded.

Jürgen was not paying attention anymore. He knew now that the vessel was foundering because it carried a man on board who had broken his pledge.

He held the wheel tightly.

Then a bright star appeared in the black distance, it floated over the waters and came closer.

Jürgen stared with wide open eyes at the blue light. Yes, now he saw it, it was the saviour who was hurrying across the water in his white robe to fetch the lost man.

The blue star glinted and flashed over his head, and the god came nearer and stretched out his hand.

Jürgen let the wheel go, and immediately his boat whirled around in a circle.

"Come," the god said, "you have sinned against me, but I am the love."

Jürgen tumbled to the side and leant over.

"Come," the apparition whispered once more, and its countenance radiated supernatural brightness. "Come."

Then Jürgen emitted a bloodcurdling scream, and sprang in fierce desire towards the mild god.

"Jürgen!" his brothers screamed.

But no answer was heard, the called man dove into that endless sea whose waves roll to eternity, and far, far away, the light of the blue star went out.

About the Publisher

Our mission is to provide translations into English of the complete works of neglected major European writers. We do not cherry-pick works that seem the most marketable, but rather seek to provide a complete collection of each writer's works so that readers can follow the writer's development and decide on its merits for themselves.

http://www.facebook.com/KANitzPublishing

http://www.kanitzpublishing.com